THE BECALMER

NICK WILFORD

Published in the United States by Creative James Media.

www.creativejamesmedia.com

978-1-956183-64-1 (trade paperback)

First U.S. Edition 2023

THE BECALMER

Novels

The Black & White trilogy:

Black & White

Corruption

Reckoning

Anthologies

A Change of Mind and Other Stories

Overcoming Adversity: An Anthology for Andrew (editor)

Full Dark: An Anthology (featuring short story The Caricature)

CONTENT WARNING

This book contains scenes of attempted sexual assault and graphic violence.

This book is dedicated to my wonderful wife, Heather, and my amazing children Andrew, Hannah, Emma and Eve. Without all of you I wouldn't have been able to sustain this writing journey over the past fifteen years.

CHAPTER 1

I suppose I should have seen it coming. After all, I'd resolved a conflict between the two highest officials in school simply by sitting between them and entering their heads. The only question was who had reported my gift to the powers that be.

My parents were happy. I was keeping my head down, just doing the do. And then came the ominous buzz at the front door.

Dad looked at the screen and reported that it was two men wearing the neat, pressed blue suits that marked them as representatives of the Narbrutsi government. The ostentatious gold insignia on their sleeves were all too visible, too. These people didn't like to go incognito, something we'd learnt from the news.

Later Dad said that he didn't immediately make the connection to what they probably wanted—if he had, he wouldn't have let them in. But that wouldn't have washed. These weren't people who gave up easily, and they'd have been back sooner rather than later.

So, in the event, he opened the door and unleashed the next chaotic chapter in our lives.

Mum and I had scuttled into the kitchen, leaving Dad to it, but the open-plan layout meant we clocked the two guys. Their appearance would have been comical if we didn't know it probably meant trouble. The one on the left was skinny with neatly trimmed blond hair, while his partner was stocky and bald with small, hooded eyes.

"Mr Spindelman?" said the man on the right, while both men held up their palms, in front of which flashed bold 3Dis, three-dimensional IDs consisting of a headshot and a readout of the bearer's credentials.

"That's me," Dad confirmed after a few moments. "How can I help you gentlemen?"

"It's a delicate matter," said the same dude who'd spoken. "We'd rather talk about it inside."

His impassive tone and demeanour implied we didn't have a lot of choice in the matter, and seeing how we didn't have anything to hide, Dad played the good citizen by nodding and gesturing for them to come in. He shut the door after the second man.

The two hovered in the living room until Dad told them to sit on the couch. Of course they'd clocked me and Mum in the kitchen thanks to the ubiquitous open-plan layout, but Mum had hastily got a couple of ingredients out so we could act like we were busy making dinner while keeping an ear on proceedings. That wasn't to be, however.

"Good evening," said the stocky man, looking in our direction. "Could I ask you two to join us? This is a matter that involves all of you."

I glanced at Dad, trying to guess what he was thinking, but he just shifted his weight from one foot to the other and nodded. What could two government goons want to speak to us for? My stomach lurched as I considered the possibilities. We came and sat on the other couch while Dad took the reclining chair, although he appeared anything but relaxed.

"Would you like anything to drink?" asked Mum, ever the diligent hostess.

The first man smiled thinly, but then shook his head. "No, we'd rather get straight down to business. Now, of course you'll be aware of the ongoing difficulties between us and the Camzhargi. There's nothing we want more than to coexist with them peacefully, but they seem intent on sabotaging every move we make. For example, this unfortunate business with Princess Jasmila and our young prince. They could have a wonderful life together, a model that other nations could follow, but thanks to her reticence, and her vague and unfounded accusation of wrongdoing, it seems destined not to be."

The slender guy leaned in and spoke for the first time. "Now we find ourselves returning to the old negotiation methods, though the upcoming talks are likely to be more fraught than ever," he said in a voice that was peculiarly high-pitched in comparison to his companion. "There is nothing new to bring to the table. We need some kind of bargaining chip or a secret weapon that would let us defuse this situation once and for all—and I don't mean a physical weapon. We don't want any more carnage on our cities' streets, and we're trying to stamp out this incessant violence for good."

"You're not doing a very good job of it," said Dad.

The man raised an eyebrow at this blunt intrusion but made no other response. Probably against protocol to speak out of turn like that with a government official, but this was Dad's house and it was our peace that had been disturbed. Our moon was neutral—in theory we had nothing to do with this, so why had we let these two across our threshold? *Good on you, Dad.*

The one who seemed to be in charge picked up the thread again.

"We need something more where diplomacy has failed." His gaze locked straight onto mine, and I returned it with my best deadbeat stare. "We have heard about your, uh, impressive gift—although we're not sure if your parents are aware of it," he added as if checking himself.

I rolled my eyes. "They are. I don't keep things from my parents, so don't worry about betraying any secrets. But who blabbed to you? Was it Mrs Jangaman? Because you sound a lot like she did when she asked for my help not long ago. Tell me, why can't you adults resolve your problems on your own without getting a little girl to intervene?"

Before the goon could reply, Dad cut in. "What do you know about Harica's talents?"

That's right, Daddy, discuss my attributes like I'm a prize race plug. It's like I'm not even in the room.

The first man said, "We know she has the power to mediate disputes using only her mind."

I snorted. "There's more to it than that. It's about the minds of the people in the dispute—I need to get into them and take control, and if one or both of them doesn't want to let me in, I'll fail. It's not a superpower. It's not guaranteed to work, and there's a lot of times it doesn't. I don't know what you're asking me to do here, but the first time I tried doing an adult's *dispute*—as you call it—the entire contents of my stomach ejected themselves. I felt totally drained, in my mind as well as my digestive system." I shuddered as I remembered that occasion in Mrs Jangaman's office. All because she and the vice principal disagreed on a matter of discipline. Why was that down to me to sort out?

Dad stood up and took a couple of steps towards the men. "My daughter has schoolwork and responsibilities," he said, trying to loom over them—although as a man of middling height, the effect wasn't all it could have been. "She's not a secret weapon, or a bargaining chip or however else you'd like to describe her. She's a human being, and we ask that she's allowed to get on with her life in peace."

"We don't even like her to get involved in her friends' quarrels," said Mum, putting her hand over mine on the couch. "We consider it a distraction. And we don't think it's good for her health."

"Look," said the second man. "There's no guarantee it will work, of course. But your daughter's intervention could be the thing that stops any more bloodshed and innocent civilians being caught in the crossfire. Wouldn't you like her to play a key part in building a lasting legacy of peace?"

"I can speak for myself, you know," I said, trying to make eye contact with the man, although he strenuously avoided it. It was like I was invisible to the two of them. "And yeah, I'd love to help, if I thought it could make a difference. But I'm not sure I can. It might be too much for me to cope with." Truth be told, I was scared of the effects it might have, after what happened in the principal's office. I didn't want to give myself an aneurysm or something.

But being able to make a difference to the future of the planet? That wasn't something I should pass up lightly, was it? And what if the conflict spread to our own home in the future?

"You heard her," said Dad, standing up, ready to usher

the two men on their way. "Our daughter's health is paramount here."

The fair headed guy looked to the guy in charge, who gave a very slight shrug of his shoulders, and then looked back at Dad, pinning him with an icy stare. "I wouldn't think of this as over yet. If only there was a way your daughter's talent could be harnessed without the adverse effects on her health. Get in touch if you change your mind." He produced a card with contact details and set it on the table.

"Good day to you," said Dad in his overly formal way, clearly unwilling to engage in any further dialogue. "You can see yourselves out."

Both men stood up and made their way to the door, although not before the one in charge caught my eye and gave a knowing look as if to acknowledge that my own feelings weren't quite as unequivocal as my dad's. I just stared back blankly until the door closed behind them.

"I think we need to move to another planet," said Dad.

"Now dear, there's no need to be so dramatic," said Mum. "They'll find us wherever we are. If they ever come back, we just do the same thing—whatever they want us to do, we just politely, but firmly, decline."

We? There's no we here, Mum—I'm the one they're after. Of course, fat chance of being asked my opinion on the matter. I shook my head and scooted up to my room, but not before scooping up the card left on the table, getting no objections from my parents—of course, to them I was clearly invisible, like with that man, and they probably didn't think I would actually contact them.

Closing the door behind me, I paced up and down for a minute before throwing myself on the bed, but nothing helped me process my thoughts. A tidal wave of conflicting emotions was threatening to engulf me. I knew one thing—I couldn't just dismiss the chance to make a difference to millions of people and potentially prevent countless casualties. My parents might have ruled the idea out flat, but that didn't mean I had.

CHAPTER 2

At school the next morning, I continued to turn down any requests to mediate in petty squabbles. It wasn't out of deference to my parents' wishes, flam no—I just had the vague feeling I should conserve my energy in case I did decide to take up those men on their offer. Which was totally my right to do. If I wanted.

At morning recess, I was going through the virtual books on my EduPad in readiness for the next class when Miriam, my bestie since we were both in year zero, sidled up. I was just done brushing off a guy who wanted me to intervene in his dispute with his dad over him getting a solarbike. I had my own issues with the parentals—I didn't need his—so it was a relief to speak to someone who wasn't coming at me with an ulterior motive.

"What's up?" she said, adjusting her bag on her shoulder and giving me a once-over with eyes that were full of warmth. "You look stressed."

"That obvious, huh?" I pinged a thick textbook on the history of Euripidean mining to the front of the queue for Interplanetary Geology. It would be full of dry-as-Jovandust facts and figures, but anything was better with my bestie at my side.

"I thought you were feeling better now you were laying off the mediations," she said, scrolling through her own device.

"Hey, that's not the only thing that might worry me, okay?" I said, slipping my pad into my bag and shrugging it onto my shoulders. She gave me a sideways look through the long purple hair that framed her face, and I sighed.

"Sorry, I didn't mean to snap like that. Something's happened . . . well, something's come up, and I don't feel like I can talk about it here," I said, eyeing the mass of kids buzzing around us. "Come over tonight, we can hang out and I'll tell you all about it. But this stays between us, okay?"

She turned to me, arms folded and head tipped to one side. "And when has that ever not been the case?"

"Hey, you're right, I'm sorry." I sighed, reaching out and touching her on the shoulder. "I don't know what I was thinking." I felt like I was in other people's business all the time, even going right inside their heads, but I didn't share my own issues easily. Miriam was the only person I could really trust, and I had no right questioning that.

"So, what's going on with you?" I said as we walked to class, eager to deflect the attention away from myself.

"Oh, just the same old, same old," she said, shaking her head. "Dunyon's being a douche again, saying I never make time for him anymore."

"Hey, the work's getting intense now we're in year thirteen, and you need to study like the good little girl you are. Just because his grades are bottoming out and he's probably only going to make it as a sidewalk scrubber," I snorted. The sidewalks on our moon were made of a smooth, slightly bouncy but ultra-strong synthetic material, which guarded against injury. They wiped clean easily, but someone had to do that, and that was grunt work.

I felt for Miriam. Unlike plain ol' me, she'd blossomed into a drop-dead beauty during our time at school, and she hadn't been without a boyfriend for the past three years, but in my humble opinion, not a single one of them had been worthy of her radiance. Deadbeat Dunyon was certainly no exception.

"He's messaged me to hang tonight. I could have made the time, I mean we need to hook up so we can work through what's going on between us, but I'll postpone. My bestie needs me. Boys come second."

I grinned. I was glad I could always rely on Miriam to have my back, and what was more, she'd never once asked me to use my gift to intervene in her dramas. She knew other people exploited it without a second thought, and that it could take a lot out of me.

Miriam came round about nine that night. I'd been sitting with my parents in the living room so I could get to the door first. "I'll get it," I said, jumping up when I heard the door chime. I didn't bother with the interface that let us see who was on the other side, opening the door quickly and ushering her in. She'd changed out of her more elegant school attire but still looked effortlessly chic.

"Miriam's here to do homework," I shouted. My folks waved their greetings through the living room door, and Miriam and I trooped upstairs. I hadn't told them she'd be coming, but it wasn't unusual for us to hang at each other's houses, we just hadn't done much of it recently.

"So, what's going on? I can tell something's been bothering you," she said once we were settled in my room, Miriam on the bed while I took the desk chair. It was typical of her to get straight to the point.

"Well . . . it's pretty big," I said, fiddling with my favourite desk toy, a miniature monkey swinging on a vine in a wooden frame. "Massive, actually. Seems like word has spread outside the school about my talent."

Miriam sat forward, a frown briefly passing across her face. "Not totally surprising. Something like that is pretty hard to keep hidden, and how many kids have you helped? I think we've lost count, haven't we?"

"Yeah. And I told you about the principal, didn't I?" I said, looking up from the monkey and catching her eye.

"That was totally ridiculous, and I said so at the time." She sat back against the headboard, crossing her arms and shaking her head briefly.

"I know you did. So, you're not going to like the next development," I said, still holding her somewhat baleful gaze.

"Come on, let's hear it. Massive, you said."

"Yeah. Well, these two guys showed up at the door, suited up, turned out they were from the government down on the planet. Basically, they want me to intervene in the war between the Camzhargi and the Narbrutsi, stop all the fighting that's going on."

Her eyes widened. "Woah. That's, like . . . Would you even be able to do something like that? What effect is it going to have on you?"

"That's the thing, I don't know until I try. Of course, my parents are dead set against it. You know I vommed after the thing with Jangaman, that was some intense stuff. But, you know, I'm not totally decided one way or the other. That's why I wanted to ask you."

"Well, it's way too much. You can't be seriously considering it? Something like that could . . . well, it could kill you!" She looked at the door and added, "Sorry," in a much lower voice, as if worried we could be overheard.

"I don't know." I leaned forward, whispering in return. "I know it's a big risk and everything, but at the same time I feel like . . . this could be my moment, you know? My destiny. Millions of lives are at stake and look how many have already been lost. This thing is bigger than me, and maybe I would be selfish to say no just to protect myself."

"I get that, I do, but we're not talking some fallout over a stolen homework assignment here. There's some deep-down hatred behind all this. How are you even going to handle that?"

I sighed. "I'm not sure, but . . . maybe I need to have better control over my power. Not let it consume *me*, drain me in the process. There's no one else I can ask for help with that, it's got to come from inside me. I've been avoiding intervening in anyone's squabbles lately, and maybe that's all drassic if I'm going to do this. I need to not let my resources get used up."

She stared at the geometric patterns on the bedsheet. "I don't know. I suppose only you know what you're capable of, but . . ."

"Or maybe I don't," I cut in. "Maybe I'm still discovering that. Maybe I just need to see how far I can push it."

"Let's talk practically for a minute," she said, looking up. "You said your parents are totally against this? How would you be able to get away without them knowing?"

She'd hit on the biggest sticking point if I was actually

going to do this. "Well, I'd need to go behind their backs. Not something I want to be doing, but . . . " I drifted off into my thoughts.

Miriam looked me dead in the eyes. "I know what I just said, that it's too much, but . . . I can't see there's a choice. If you passed up a chance to save millions of lives, could you forgive yourself for that?"

I held her gaze for a few moments, but then broke it, letting go an involuntary giggle. This was no laughing matter, but the enormity of the situation felt too much to take in.

"I don't even need to think about that," I said. "No, I couldn't."

Miriam sat forward on the bed, a light seeming to click on in her eyes. "Look, I see their point of view. I don't want you to put yourself in harm's way, whatever the reason, but what if the answer's staring us in the face? There must be a way to get their approval."

"What . . ." I started, and then stopped and thought about it, encouraged by Miriam's frantic nodding and eyebrow-raising to see what was right in front of me. My parents and I were in conflict. And resolving conflicts was kind of my forte.

"I don't know . . . That seems like a misuse to me. Too close to home. I don't want to use my gift against my parents for my own ends . . . And how does it work if *I'm* one of the parties to the dispute? What would happen?"

"There's no way of knowing that, I guess. Maybe that's part of exploring this thing, seeing where you can take it. Anyway, it's not for your own ends. You've got to stop beating yourself up that you'd be selfish by doing this. It's totally selfless . . . totally brave." She gave me one of her dazzling smiles, which never failed to lift my spirits.

"I get that, I do, but . . . no, I can't do that to them," I decided. "They don't like me using it at the best of times, so I'd need to do it without them knowing, and that's far too sneaky. It's off the table."

She shrugged, using just her right shoulder. "Then if you're going to win them round, the only way to do it is the old-school way. I can back you up if you like. Maybe a third party would be a good idea, help them see things from an outsider's view."

"That's sweet of you, but . . ." Why did this idea seem wrong to me too? I had always been the one offering others my help, expecting absolutely nothing in return. Maybe I could use a little help myself.

"But what? Come on, this is too important. You don't want to always be wondering whether you could have made a difference. The war doesn't show any sign of stopping by itself, does it?"

I took an intense interest in the floor. Maybe I could do it if I had Miriam's help. My parents had always got on with her, after all. But when I failed to say anything else, Miriam continued, "We could go downstairs and tell them now, if you like."

That idea made me totally clam up, and I hemmed and hawed a bit before saying, "Ummm . . . I just need a little more time. Can you come over tomorrow night?"

"Sure! Dunyon's messaging me for us to go on a date—turbo rollerblading, would you believe it—but I can put him off again. Anything for my bestie, and this is a priority."

I grinned, happy that I could rely on Miriam to have my back. As much as I disliked Dunyon, I felt bad about coming between them, because I knew Miriam liked him. Another reason why it was important not to stall on this any more than I had already done. I'd have the whole of the next day to build myself up to it, and I had to use that time well.

Miriam hung out for a little while longer and we chatted about unrelated stuff like the latest music we were into—Miriam liked Radiohead, but I'd never warmed to classical music—and which of our teachers was the most likely to have a nervous breakdown. By the time I eventually got into bed, the butterflies in my stomach from the thought of confronting my parents had calmed down a bit, and it felt like it was simply an obstacle that had to be overcome on the path to some sort of—what, destiny? Whatever it was, I felt like I was being called by something bigger than myself, and I didn't think I could forgive *myself* if I didn't at least give it a shot.

CHAPTER 3

The next day brought with it news of further chaos
down on the planet, which was unavoidable to
anyone who sat and scrolled through the platforms even for
a minute. There'd been an ambush the previous afternoon
on a group of Camzhargi civilians who hadn't done
anything wrong. They'd been on their way to a christening,
and just the presence of them en masse had been enough to
antagonize a squad of militant Narbrutsi, who killed fifteen
out of the twenty-two—including elderly citizens—and
injured a further four. Those who managed to escape told
their story to the media.

All because Jasmila Camzhargi was refusing to enter
into a marriage that had been brokered between her and
Prince Narbert of the Narbrutsi, claiming to have some
unspecified dirt on him. I wouldn't like being forced into an
arranged marriage either, but who would drag their feet
over a chance to save millions of lives? I didn't know
everything about the princess, obviously, but "selfish"
seemed to be the overwhelming vibe that came from her.

Anyway, surely this was going to help my case with my

parents. They'd have to take a good long look at themselves if they denied me the opportunity to try to prevent any more gut-wrenching mayhem like this. But then, we already knew about such incidents when those guys came to the door, and they didn't leap at the chance then. Why couldn't they see how important it was that I had to try this?

In the middle of a day that seemed to be moving at the speed of your average glacier, Miriam and I discussed the latest events over lunch in the cafeteria.

"This is barbaric stuff, man," she said, in between mouthfuls of hot choi stew. I had to smile at the fact it didn't put her off her food—nothing could. I was always slightly jealous of the fact she could put away what she liked and not have it affect her enviable model figure. "A bunch of innocent citizens on their way to church, most of them way into their eighties. If that doesn't shake up their conscience, what will?"

"I don't know. My parents are pretty stubborn," I said, my own plate sitting mostly untouched in front of me, evidence of my nerves over the impending showdown. "They don't want to put their only child in harm's way, but I'm hardly a child anymore. I can handle it."

Miriam gestured with one hand while finishing another mouthful of stew. She swallowed and said, "Okay, so what if we can use that angle somehow? Turn it around? Each of these victims most likely had a family—children, grandchildren, greatgrandchildren. Let's see if we can get some more detail on them, make it more personal." She waved the fingers of her right hand over her left palm to activate the infochip implanted there, and I did the same. We both pointed at the same news icon with our fingers and started scrolling through a story about the attack. The author had been quite exhaustive in their work—part of the story included mini profiles and photos of most of the victims, which you could project and examine in more detail.

"Look at this sweet old guy," she said, pulling up a photo showing a good-natured, rosy-cheeked old man reclining in an upholstered armchair. "Cecily Sandalbridge, ninety-three-years old, five children, twelve grandchildren. Ah, man. The christening was for his first great-granddaughter. What's anyone stand to gain by killing him? What point are they making?" She glanced up from the photo, and our eyes locked. Hers were moistening—it didn't take a lot to get Miriam emotional. "If it's not pushing things too much, maybe ask how they'd feel if it was one of your grandparents that was caught up in this."

I gulped, despite the lack of food in my mouth. "I don't think that would go down well," I said, even though fortunately, my remaining grandparents were safely holed up in neighbouring towns to ours and not on the surface of Planet Hellhole. "We can make it personal, but not *that* personal."

"Okay, understood," she said, shrugging slightly. We went back to studying the profiles, in silence this time, looking for anything that, for want of a better word, could be considered "juicy." And boy, did I get it. There was something familiar about the tiny thumbnail even before I clicked on it, despite the lack of definition, and when I read the story, I struggled to take in what my eyes were seeing.

"Mauritz Spindelman, eighty-seven," I read out, and Miriam's head snapped up at the mention of my own surname. Her fingers worked the readout to quickly bring up the same part of the story. "He lived alone, no children, but he'd been in the area for forty-six years and was well liked and respected in the community." I studied the photo again, shaking my head at what looked like an exact double of my dad with the addition of some wrinkles, white hair and a pair of thin-framed glasses. Surely the coincidence would have been too great. This wasn't my grandfather, I knew that much, so was I looking at my great-uncle or some sort of distant cousin? How come I knew nothing about this guy?

My mind started spinning into overdrive as it attempted to process what I was seeing. Meanwhile, Miriam started vocalizing my exact first thoughts.

"Whoever he is, if he's a relation of yours, this could be just the leverage you need," she said, her voice taking on a more urgent tone. "Surely now your folks will see you have to try and do this—it just got personal. Hell, if you'd left when those guys first came to your house, you could have prevented it." I watched her face while still trying to process my own racing thoughts, and it shifted into a frown as if she was trying to think of something else she was supposed to say. "Hey . . . I'm sorry for your loss."

"Scratch that," I said, waving a hand. "I didn't know the guy, so it's not like I can mourn. You're right, I need to be looking at this in terms of how it can help my case, but I dunno . . . something seems off to me. *Why* didn't I know about this guy? My parents never mentioned him. That can't be right."

Miriam shrugged. "A lot of people have folks they never see, or who don't even come up in conversation. Maybe you did hear about him when you were a lot younger, and you've just forgotten. Do your folks have a large extended family?"

My parents were insular as all hell, but that didn't mean there weren't relatives out there. "Not that I really know about. My mum has a brother and sister, we last saw them a couple of years ago at Christmas. My dad, though . . . he's an only child, like me. At least, as far as I know, and why would he lie about that? This guy has my dad's name."

Miriam sat back and raised one side of her mouth slightly. "Then he's probably a distant third cousin, twice removed, or something like that."

This was getting more tenuous by the minute. "What if *they've* forgotten he exists? They could see this story, see the name, but it doesn't really have any effect on them, at least not enough to let me go. He lived down planetside, and we know they're dead set against going there, so it's not like they would have been in touch much."

"Hey, blood is blood. There's probably a good reason they never saw him and living planetside seems to fit the bill. There's going to be some sort of connection, some history there. We have to use this."

"Okay." I nodded, trying to convince myself. I looked at the screen again, captivated by the image of Mauritz, and saw what my dad might become. If this didn't work, nothing would.

▭

When I got home that afternoon, Dad was at work, and Mum was streaming some interplanetary romance in the living room. Normally I would shout through a quick greeting and head upstairs, but today I flumped in the armchair just across from where she sat on the couch. I kicked off my shoes and reclined the seat, trying to act as normal as possible while attempting to quiet what seemed like a whole colony of butterflies flitting around my insides. *So not looking forward to later.*

"Did you have a good day, dear?" said Mum, briefly looking away from the screen.

"Yeah. Hey, Mum, can Miriam come for dinner tonight?"

"Well, let me see, I'm sure I can rustle up an extra helping of Carvissian stew. What time is she coming?"

"About six," I said, fiddling with my sleeves.

"I'm glad you've got a good friend, dear. Keeps you occupied," she said, and although she didn't elaborate, we both knew she was referring to the use of my gift—a megadon in the room that not only seemed to fill up all the space between us, but might as well have been trumpeting a selection of jazz classics and balancing on one foreleg.

I had no way of knowing if she or Dad had seen the story about the mysterious Mauritz. If she had, and it meant something to her, maybe she wasn't mentioning it because she didn't think it would mean anything to me. If that was the case, I disagreed. The death of any family member should be something you know about, even if you never knew of their existence before. Well, I'd be breaking that seal tonight. Shifting uncomfortably in my seat as that thought became a physical sensation oozing its way stickily through my body, I slammed down the reclining part of the chair with my feet and stood up quickly. "Well, I've got a bit of homework to do before Miriam gets here. Thanks again, Mum." I hopped over to her seat and gave her a quick peck on the cheek.

"No problem," she called, but I was already beating a retreat, through the door and upstairs to my room.

Mum called up to me when Miriam arrived, and I trooped downstairs while a flood of adrenaline washed through me. I'd been distracted by my work for a couple of hours, but now it was time to make my play.

We all sat around the table making slightly stilted conversation about how things were going at school in between mouthfuls of stew. I found it hard to taste mine as I contemplated raising the subject of what was going on planetside—I remembered the last time all too well. But when we'd finished, and Mum suggested getting out the dessert, Dad said it would be better to let the stew digest for a while. I took that as my cue to change the subject.

"Hey, did you hear there was another attack down on the surface yesterday?" I tried to sound as light as possible, but I probably sounded a bit strangled.

Mum first flinched and then stiffened. Dad remained motionless, then took a slow and deliberate gulp of water and said, "Yes, of course. I hardly think it's a suitable topic for pleasant dinner conversation though."

"Maybe, but we can't pretend it's not happening. Really, I'm only mentioning it because I saw the name of one of the victims. Hang on," I said and activated my infochip, feeling my parents' eyes burning a hole in my head while I pulled up the story and Mauritz's picture. "Here. Do you recognize this man?" I said, projecting it out to them. "His name was Mauritz Spindelman."

They both went as still as statues. Mum's eyes dropped from me to her empty plate, but Dad's continued their mission to penetrate my soul. A few cloying seconds passed where it felt like we were in a compression chamber, with the air bearing down on us.

"You don't need to worry about things like this. It doesn't concern us," Dad said finally in a monotone.

"Doesn't concern us?" My other hand grasped the air. "I've never heard of anyone else with our name before. Is he a relation? Does he mean anything to you?"

"No," said Dad, while Mum remained perfectly still.

"And if you think this is a reason to let you go on some fool's mission down to that planet, you're wrong. I don't want to hear anything about this stupid 'gift' again, or whatever you call it. You've got a good life here, and I won't see you put yourself in danger."

"*Fine*," I said too loudly, "but there's something you're not telling me, I know it. I can't believe you've got no compassion and you're willing to stand by while people die. Even maybe one of our family. I need to get some air."

I scraped my chair back and rose unsteadily from the table before finding my feet and dashing out the front door. As I was drawing in a deep intake of breath, the door opened again, and Miriam joined me. She didn't say anything, just let me collect myself for a few moments.

"I knew it, there's more to this," I said eventually. "They wouldn't tell me about Mauritz, but that says a lot itself. If there were no issues, they'd have told me about him quite happily. I'd probably have heard about him before; in fact, they'd probably have brought the subject up to me rather than the other way round."

"That makes sense," she said. "There must have been something that happened in the past that they've basically wiped from history. So they're refusing to talk?"

"Do you think it's to do with my gift?" I said, turning to look at her. "That'd be a definite reason for Dad putting his foot down. Maybe Mauritz had the same thing or there's some other link."

"It's possible. We're not going to find out from your folks though, that's clear."

"Yeah." I laughed harshly. "You know what though, it only makes me more determined. Maybe I'll find out more about Mauritz if I go down there, and more about myself. And every single one of those victims, their death is going to affect someone. They're not just numbers. We've got to do this."

"Okay." She nodded. "We'll work out what we're going to do, but remember I've got your back the whole way."

"Thanks."

After Miriam hugged me and took off, I headed back inside and went straight upstairs, seeing my parents out of the corner of my eye still sitting at the dinner table like mannequins but refusing to look their way. Honestly, could they be any more selfish? Here I had a chance to actually make a difference to millions of people's lives—or actually save their lives—and they just couldn't see it. It was like they were just blocking out the outside world. They were concerned about my safety, I got that, but I wasn't a kid anymore. I could look after myself. Hopefully I would have Miriam on my side too, though I wasn't sure she would be able to get away from her mum either.

I brushed my teeth roughly, spitting out the toothpaste like I was getting rid of the closeted life I was leading. After I'd finished, I regarded my reflection and, on some level, I looked like who I knew I was—your typical sulky teen, yada yada, a flamming cliché made flesh . . . but maybe also more than that.

Someone who was waiting to fulfil her destiny, who had a higher purpose.

And if defying my parents was what I had to do to make that happen, then so be it.

CHAPTER 4

Next morning, I woke with a clear head and a sense of inner calm, despite the difficult situation I was in. I'd passed out almost as soon as my head hit the pillow and clocked up a solid eight hours, which never happened for me—it always took me a while to get to sleep, and although it was worse at some times than others, those liminal moments between consciousness and oblivion tended to be when all the bad mojo I'd sucked into my brain from defusing others' drama tended to rear its head and camp out in my cortex, like a negativity-fest that invaded my dreams. I'd had none of that last night. I had no doubt it'd be back, but maybe I could learn to better control it so it didn't control me—I was going to have to if I had any chance of stopping a war. And I didn't know how yet, but it was clear to me that Mauritz was the key to this. He might be gone from this world, but I was going to do all I could to find out more about him and this gift that seemed so similar to my own.

I pulled up the VirPad from my infochip and tapped in

the ID from the bit of paper those guys left the other day. I knew I'd have to do this before the air of bravado I'd woken up with deserted me. With my fingers shaking a tiny bit, I put together a message on the floating display and hit "Send."

That was it. Fate officially sealed. Next, on what looked likely to be my last day at school for an indefinite period, I had to work on Miriam.

The first couple of lessons, Astronomy and Geo-Economics, I could barely focus to take anything in. As the words on the EduPad swam in front of me, I knew breaktime would be the first chance I'd get to properly talk to her. And although, unlike my parents, I knew she'd always have my back, convincing her to uproot her life for an unknown length of time and follow me into the heart of a war zone was going to be a massive ask, to say the least.

While we were swapping books between classes, I told Miriam I was going.

She looked up at me with eyebrows raised. "Really? Your parents came round?"

"No."

"Okay then, how . . ." She stopped and gave a small grin. The look in her eyes told me she already had the answer.

I sighed and shook my head as I finished organizing my things. "They can't make my decisions for me. On some moons you're legally an adult when you're sixteen."

"Not this one, though," she said, scratching her chin with one immaculately manicured thumbnail.

"That's an accident of birth, and so's being born with this gift or talent or whatever you want to call it," I muttered. "I never asked for it. But maybe the whole reason it's there is because of this moment. I have to do this with or without my parents' approval."

She smiled. "I don't know if I'd have your confidence."

"You're the most confident person I know." I had to ask her before I lost my nerve. The moment would be gone once we slipped back into the morass of classes for the rest of the day. I was about to take the plunge when she spoke again.

"So, how are you going to get away from them?"

"Those guys that came to the house, they're going to pick me up a few blocks away, five tomorrow morning. Then I'll message my parents, but only once I'm on my way. Any sooner and it'll be impossible, they'll probably lock me in my room and feed me bread and water."

"You're a badass, Harica, I like this side of you," she said, nodding. "But aren't you worried they'll come after you?"

I looked to the left and right, as if they were somewhere around, listening. "That's why I'm going to make sure I'm well away first. I'll do it from the shuttle, hopefully that's going to be early enough they'll still be sleeping. It's just to let them know I'm doing this of my own free will, that I haven't been abducted or anything, and that they have to let me do this. Also, that I'm not going to be on my own."

We'd started to move off to the next class while I was speaking, so at first I wasn't sure Miriam registered that last sentence. Then she pulled up short and turned to me with her brown eyes completely round. "Wait . . . what? Who's going with you?"

In response, I simply lifted my eyebrows, gave a very faint nod and offered the ghost of a smile.

She just stared back at me and then put her hand to her chest and burst out laughing. "You want me . . . to come? To Camzhargi?"

I took her other hand and squeezed it. "Doesn't it make

sense? We've been through everything together, our whole lives. There's no one I'd rather have at my side now."

She composed herself, nodding a few times quickly. "Okay, so I guess you're not joking. But I mean, shoot, Harica . . . what about Mum? What about school? What about everything?"

"Don't think I haven't thought about it all. And if we both go at the same time then I know they're going to be onto us. I just can't see if you came later that we'd even be able to meet, I just don't know how it's going to go. It's kind of now or never."

"Okay. So . . . when do you go again?"

"Tomorrow. First thing. Could you come for a sleepover tonight?"

"Um . . ." She tucked her hair behind her ear and looked down at the floor for a moment, smiling briefly again. "Sure, Harica, I can do that. But there's a lot of unknowns here, you know? What if they don't let me come with you? And what am I going to tell my mum?"

"We'd better get to class, don't want to be late," I said, jerking my head. "Don't want to arouse suspicion." As we walked, I said, "Look, I'll message them today, say I need to have my best friend with me or everything's off. And you're absolutely to be trusted. I mean hell, Miriam, I'd trust you with my life, probably more than my parents. And as for your mum, I mean, well . . ."

"Yeah, I know what you're thinking," she said. "And you'd be right. She'd hardly miss me because she wants to spend all her time with Brian, well, that is until it goes sour, then she'll move on to the next schmuck," she snorted. "But anyway. I can tell her I'm moving in with you for a while. She's not going to look into that any further or check in with your folks or anything, so that should cover us."

"Thanks." I squeezed her arm. "Looks like we're set, then."

"Set to go into the unknown," she said.

CHAPTER 5

I hardly slept that night for thinking of what the next day would bring. I didn't want the alarm waking my parents up at four in the morning, so I brought up the clock readout above my palm and stared at it for long stretches of time, watching the minutes slowly tick by. Miriam dozed fitfully on the camp bed on the floor of my room, and in between times we'd whisper words of encouragement—mini pep talks, I guess, for the massive upheaval we were about to unleash on our lives. I don't think either of us had fully grasped the implications or the enormity of it yet.

At five to four, I deactivated the alarm and peeled myself out of bed. I stretched, trying to get some life into my aching muscles. I should have been exhausted after hardly sleeping, but instead I felt wired, buzzed, whatever you want to call that feeling like electricity coursing through your body. I shook Miriam gently on the shoulder and she snorted, still in one of her dozing phases.

"Ssh," I cautioned. "It's time to go."

After opening her eyes, she looked at me and blinked as

if she couldn't work out what I was doing there. She gave a lazy smile and yawned before swinging her legs off the cot.

"Oh, wow," she said, a look of realization widening her eyes. "Are we really doing this?"

"Yes, and we'd better keep the noise down," I whispered. "Last thing we want is to be caught now."

"I was just getting into a proper sleep at the end there," she murmured. "Just kept thinking about it all before that. It feels like we're fugitives . . . breaking the law, or something."

"I know," I said, as I dressed hurriedly in a dark blue miflon suit. "But we're actually doing something that could save millions—we could be the heroes in all this."

"Well, it's you that'll be doing the heroing. I'm just tagging along."

"It's essential that you're there," I said, looking in her eyes and nodding. "You've got my back, and I couldn't do it without you."

And it was true. I felt much more reassured knowing Miriam was at my side, where she had always been, than if I was throwing myself into this completely alone and vulnerable.

We both got ready in silence, knowing my parents were just a couple of rooms away. I switched on the desk lamp instead of the overhead light just in case one of them got up to go to the bathroom and saw the light under the door. I scraped my brush through my hair and pulled it back into a loose ponytail, and Miriam did something similar, the vibe being practical rather than stylish.

I finished packing a few essential toiletries into the bag I'd packed last night. We slung our bags over our shoulders and crept downstairs.

Just as I was using my palm to open the front door, I

heard something that made my stomach sink down to about the level of my toes.

"What's going on?"

Our chance of escape gone for now, we turned to face my dad coming down the stairs. He'd been in the upstairs bathroom and heard us, I guess. Didn't matter. What was important now was talking our way out of this.

"Oh, hi Dad," I said, leaning against the doorframe, trying to act all casual-like.

"What's all this?" In contrast, he stood ramrod straight, head tilted back as if looking down his nose at us, eyes narrowed to slits. He'd have clocked the overstuffed bags and distinct lack of school uniforms.

"Off to school, Dad," I said as brazenly as I could.

His eyes narrowed so much I couldn't make out his pupils. "At this time of the morning?"

"Um, yeah," I blustered, looking at Miriam. "We've got a special project. Need to go in early because we've been put in charge."

Miriam nodded fervently.

"Why didn't you tell me before?" Dad seemed to relax just a fraction, uncrossing his arms and putting his hands in the pockets of his bathrobe.

"The decision came late yesterday. And then we were just sitting, trying to plan stuff. We were excited! But yeah, I should have told you and Mum." I tried for the cute, contrite daughter thing, putting my head to the side and looking at him through my eyelashes.

"What's the project?" he asked, seemingly unmoved by this ploy.

I'd bought myself a few seconds because this would inevitably be asked and had managed to come up with something. "It's a play," I said. "We've been put in charge of direction so we're going in before school to sort some things out, you know, brainstorming and all that. There isn't any other time to do it. And our uniforms are in our bags, we can get changed before lessons start, this is just so we can be comfy."

Dad didn't say anything for several agonisingly slow seconds, but I could see the machinery working. It was the way his left eyelid twitched slightly. No doubt he was thinking about that forbidden excursion planetside, but Miriam was a good buffer here. Why would she be involved in something so dangerous?

"Okay," he said at last, giving a very subtle nod. "Good luck." With that, he turned and started shuffling up the stairs, and Miriam and I beat a retreat while we still had the opportunity.

The car was a few blocks away, and now we would be late, which wasn't the best start. "That was close," Miriam muttered as we hurried along.

"Too close," I said. "Do you think he really bought it?"

"Honestly? I don't know. I'm sorry I wasn't any help back there, but it's your dad, you know? I thought you were best to handle it."

"It's fine," I said. "Anyway, he's going to know soon I lied to him once I send that message. The idea was just to let us get out the door. Look, there's the car." I quickened my pace, and Miriam followed suit.

The sleek black vehicle sat with its headlights on. Due to being blinded by the glare, I couldn't even check the occupants before I wrenched open the back door on the roadside, suddenly overcome by visions of my furious father pounding down the street after us. We both piled in, bags and all. I let out a breath I hadn't realized I'd been holding when I saw it was the same two men who'd come to the house that day.

"Good to see you, Miss Spindelman," said the leaner of the two, who oversaw the AI panel. He didn't turn round. "And this must be the friend you told us about?"

"Yes, this is Miriam," I said. "Look, can we get going?" I kept peering back the way we'd came, wanting to cut the chitchat and put as much distance between us and the house as possible.

"Keen, are we? That's what we like to see." I could tell he was smirking, and I just wanted this smarmy git to get moving. Finally he uttered a couple of commands, and the car pulled away from the curb. The other guy, the stocky one, hadn't said a word, and things stayed that way for the rest of the drive. Even the car had its voice mode deactivated. I was glad for the silence, although it did give me too much time to question whether I was really doing the right thing.

It took a couple of hours for the drive because we had to get to the city where the space port was located. Although I'd been to Churniston many times, I'd never been off moon before, and neither had Miriam. My skin prickled as I travelled past various familiar sights, like parks and statues, knowing I was going to leave all this behind. For how long— well, that hadn't been stated. I guessed until they were satisfied that what I was going there to do had worked. Failure was something I couldn't even entertain.

I didn't remember dozing off, but once we hit the city's outskirts, the next thing I saw was the hulking metallic mass of the spaceport as we pulled up outside it. The sun was only just starting to light the horizon, and as it rose somewhere behind the structure, it bathed it in an otherworldly glow.

Ordinarily, Miriam and I would have been chatting excitedly about our adventure and what we might do when we got to the planet, but things felt strained with these two government goons in the front, and so we'd both instinctively remained silent for almost the whole trip. I didn't know what the procedure was now, whether they'd escort us the rest of the way or hand us over to someone else. Come to think of it, I didn't know where we'd be staying when we got down there or whether there was any sort of itinerary for the job for which I was being called. I still didn't fully know what I was dealing with or what was being demanded of me, and I guess I should have been asking those questions, but I'd got a bit spooked trying to get away from my dad. Whoever was going to be our hosts for the next phase of the journey, I resolved to get some answers from them.

And I had to find out more about Mauritz, too.

"Let's go," said the driver. "Don't want to miss the flight."

We exited the vehicle quietly and started traipsing towards the imposing building. It seemed silence was expected, but it wasn't like we were under arrest, so I asked as casually as I could: "Are you guys staying with us for the rest of the journey?"

The driver—who seemed to do ninety-nine percent of the talking for the two—said, "No, we're going to hand you over to two other agents. We're moon-based operatives, we need to stay up here."

His tone wasn't unfriendly, and I thought of asking what was so pressing up here where nothing really happened, but I had a feeling that would be fruitless. Instead, I took in my surroundings. The spaceport had that functional industrial chic going on, all geometric lines and exposed concrete. It was also practically deserted. I supposed it was early yet, but the spaceport would never exactly be throbbing with travellers. It might have been in the past, but since all the trouble had started, Sintrago had lost its appeal as a destination for pleasure seekers. It was the only habitable planet in this system, and although it would have been possible to visit its other moons, they didn't offer anything substantially different to this one. So, the spaceport basically existed on an as-needed basis for government workers. It didn't do anything to support the economy—there were a few shops and restaurants dotted around the perimeter, but their metal shutters were pulled down.

We headed towards two other guys who were watching our approach. They were wearing all-in-one black flightsuits. As we got closer, I could see they were younger, probably only a few years older than us.

In fact, these guys had a different demeanour altogether. As we approached, one whispered something to the other, who sniggered, and they looked me and Miriam up and down. *Uh-uh.* They could cut that out. We were still in school, and I wasn't interested in sharing the confined space of a shuttle with two overgrown jocks buzzed on testosterone.

"Good morning," said the driver once we'd reached the two youngsters. "This is our precious cargo, Harica Spindelman, and as you know, she's got her friend Miriam Ganzapoli along for moral support. You know the mission— see them safely to where they need to be."

"You can rely on us, Agent Grythe," said one, giving me another once-over and lingering too long on my chest. *Eyes up, douchebag.* Suddenly, I was dreading this flight. I hoped it'd be over quickly and we'd be given a bit of our own space where we wouldn't be sized up like pieces of meat.

"These two young agents, Trank and Barple, have recently graduated from flight academy and are raring to go," said the one who we'd just learnt was called Grythe and who was now leaving us in the hands of these two flamheads. He nodded to each one as he said their names.

"Interesting. I assumed for our first flight there'd be experienced pilots at the helm," I jibed.

"Looks like we've got a lively one here," said Barple, offering a mirthless grin. "Come on, we'd better get going or we'll miss our flight window."

"Are there other passengers?" asked Miriam, looking around at the deserted space.

"No. You've got us all to yourselves," said Trank, leering.

"Well, like your colleague said, time is of the essence," said Grythe, oblivious, or just uncaring, about the lech-fest going on in front of his eyes. I couldn't believe it, but I didn't want the two older agents to leave. "You'd better get going. Miss Spindelman, I want to wish you the very best of luck with your mission. The welfare and very survival of this planet could be depending on it."

Yeah, maybe I should be treated with a bit more respect then. I could handle a couple of dweebs like this though, I was sure of that. Time to put on my big girl pants and deal with it.

When I didn't reply, Grythe simply nodded and said, "Goodbye then." The other agent—the one who remained nameless to us—gave a grunt, and they walked off.

Trank watched them go for a few seconds, then he turned to us and rubbed his hands together. "Your carriage awaits, ladies. Let's go."

Miriam and I exchanged glances and then trudged after them. Truth was, they—Trank in particular—probably thought they were being perfectly charming, but actually they were just creepy. At least the flight wouldn't take long. I assumed it wouldn't, although I had no real intel on that. This was a moon, and that was a planet. It wasn't like we were going to a different galaxy.

"You'll like the shuttle, it's the latest S15 Groundhopper Turbo," said Trank as we made our way deeper into the ghostly spaceport. Like that was supposed to mean anything to us. "We've taken her out a lot for exercises, and she always gives us a smooth ride. You've just got to know which buttons to press."

I screwed up my face as I felt the bile rising in my throat. He could ease up on the innuendoes right now if he wanted to press those buttons with working fingers. "Mr. Trank, or whatever you call yourself," I said faux-sweetly, "I'm here against my better judgement. I've left my home, my school" —making sure to put a bit more emphasis on that word— "and most of my friends behind. I'm going to be under immense pressure, once I get to this planet of yours, to do what I'm being asked to do, and I'm not totally sure I'm going to manage it or what it'll involve. So, would it be alright if we kept the chit-chat to a minimum? This flight might be the last bit of peace and quiet I get for a while, and I'd like to gather my thoughts."

He stopped and gave an odd mock-bow that made me want to plant my fist into his too-white teeth. "Whatever your highness requests," he drawled. "Now come on, we've got a flight window to catch."

You're the one who stopped. I thought it, but I couldn't be bothered vocalizing any more of my dislike for him. Not worth the muscle contractions it would require.

The other two were silent as we walked along in a bubble of uncomfortable atmosphere. I let out a breath I hadn't realized I'd been holding when we encountered another person at the checkpoint. The old man looked at us blearily as if we were the only people he'd seen all day. We probably were.

The two space jocks handled the formalities, handing over a small chip that I guess contained our details. We didn't have any such documentation ourselves.

After passing a few bays containing various spacecraft that had a fixed-in-place look about them, we reached the shuttle. All in black, it had a sleeker, shinier look about it that suggested it saw regular use while being well maintained. I was in no mood to appreciate the aesthetics of the thing, though. I was just dreading being in an enclosed space with these testosterone-fuelled morons.

I mean, what was so interesting about me? It wasn't like the boys were falling over themselves around me at school.

Trank removed what looked like a remote control from the pocket of his flight suit and hit a button. An unseen door opened in the hull of the craft and a set of metal steps unwound. "After you, ladies," he said, sweeping an arm towards the steep ladder-like gangway.

We didn't thank him but made our way up silently, while I tried to shake off the feeling I was being watched. Not just a feeling, I knew I was.

The inside of the vehicle was as well appointed as the outside, except instead of black, everything in here gleamed white. It was a totally open plan, so we could see the cockpit at the front with no screen or door separating us from the pilots. Oh, that was perfect. There was a large table in the middle of the space with fixed seating around it as well as comfy upholstered seats lining the walls on either side. I hoped Miriam and I could both fall asleep easily without being subjected to any more banter or whatever these flamheads wanted to call it.

"Make yourselves comfy," said Trank. "It'll take a couple of hours to reach planet side. We've got a massive library of in-flight movies as well as audiobooks for your entertainment."

"I think I'm just going to fall asleep," said Miriam, yawning. "I'm absolutely shattered." Even as she said it, she started drifting towards the nearest row of seats. With her back to me, she couldn't see the pointed look I gave her, but I gave it anyway. No way was she going to pass out and leave me vulnerable. For some reason, she'd escaped the worst of the attention from these louts, despite being stunningly gorgeous.

"Well, let's get this show on the road," said Trank, turning to his compadre. "Barple here will be your main pilot. I'll be co-pilot, making sure all systems are functioning properly, but I'll also be coming round to make sure you've got everything you need. Your comfort is uppermost in our minds during your time with us." He raised his eyebrows at me and grinned.

In response, I threw him some serious eye roll and said, "Look, can we cut the crap? We're not off for two weeks of sunning ourselves in Vodvharzi, this is a serious mission and we just want to be treated with respect. For me, that means you staying up there" —I nodded towards the cockpit— "and letting us get a bit of sleep and some chill time because I don't know what we're walking into once we get down here. Does all of that make sense to you?"

He spread his arms wide and took a couple of steps back. "Sheesh, just trying to be a gracious host and this is what I get," he said. "Okay well, as you wish, we'll keep to ourselves. You won't even know we're here."

"Sounds good to me." I turned to the side without looking at him any further and sat down next to Miriam, dumping my bag on the floor next to hers. She was nodding already, and I closed my own eyes to reinforce that there was to be no more conversation, although I didn't actually plan on sleeping. I still wanted to be on my guard because every inch of me was screaming not to trust Trank.

I heard them moving in the direction of the cockpit. Hopefully that meant an end to the nonsense.

I wanted to decompress by talking to Miriam about my fears, but I didn't feel like I could talk freely in the cramped space because they would be listening. A soft whistling sound meant she was already sleeping anyway. I cranked one eye open to see her spread oddly across two seats—it looked uncomfortable—while up ahead, the two douchebags were busying themselves at the controls and showing a semblance of professionalism. Maybe I was worrying about nothing. A steady hum started that must have been the engines roaring into life, and the craft juddered slightly as it lifted off, straight up into the air. Just a shame there weren't any windows to see out of. Up ahead, I had a narrow view through the windows of the cockpit, which only showed the walls and other features of the spaceport. I didn't know how long it took to get out of here, but when I looked away and looked back again, all I could see was blackness punctuated by faint pinpricks of light. We were on our way.

I wanted to go up to the cockpit and really take in the view of my first journey into space, but there was no way I was going up there with the pilots we were saddled with. Miriam was still slumped over, snoring faintly, and the two slimeballs were thankfully keeping themselves quiet. Normally, at this time, I'd still be sleeping myself . . . I leaned back and closed my eyes, although I tried to keep myself awake by visualizing all the scenarios that could play out once we got down there.

I must have drifted off despite my best intentions, because I was woken by the pressure of a meaty hand on my thigh. I started to scream, but the culprit clamped his other hand over my mouth once he saw I'd gained consciousness. My eyes took in Trank's sweaty, sneering face, and I tried to twist myself out from under him, but he had me pretty well pinned down.

"Don't struggle," he grunted. "Don't you want this? There's something between us, don't tell me you don't feel it too."

Shit. What could I do?

Maybe I could use my mind. My mind was my weapon, wasn't it? It might still be happening but I didn't have to feel it, if I could put myself beside the pool at Crantargo instead, soaking up the rays . . .

As I was journeying into myself, I found something that offered resistance. It was small, dense, and pulsating with malevolence. There was something . . . *greasy* about it. That seems like an odd description, but it was the overwhelming impression I got.

Could this be . . .? Had I stumbled across Trank's mind?

It hit me. This was how I could get out of this. There was a disagreement here. Trank wanted to violently assault me, and I didn't want him to. And conflict resolution via the mind was my speciality. I just hadn't known I could do it when one of the parties involved was me.

Right, no time to think on it further. This was happening. While continuing to keep my body completely rigid so he couldn't access my most vulnerable area, I launched a counterattack on his mind, teasing out the strands of ill will and placating whatever deranged motivations were behind this. It wasn't easy, like trying to physically restrain a bucking horse, but as I worked at it, I found that his mind was weaker than his body. Little surprise, really. I was able to get it under control in what must have been a few minutes—though with the effort I exerted it felt like hours—and then I felt the pressure on my body disappear.

When I opened my eyes, I saw him backing away, looking completely horror-stricken.

"What am I doing? What . . . what *was* I doing?" Shaking, he looked at me then down at his hands as if they were alien appendages.

I shrugged and raised one eyebrow slightly. "You don't remember?"

"I . . . I do remember, but I don't know why I was doing it." He couldn't seem to meet my eyes and instead focused on a spot on the floor somewhere short of my feet.

"Well," I coughed daintily, "looks like you came to your senses. After all, if I was to report something like that, it'd probably put a bit of a dampener on an otherwise promising career, wouldn't it?"

His face fell. He looked like a prepubescent boy who'd been caught with his hand in his mum's purse, but there was no way in this universe I was going to feel sorry for him. "You're going to report me."

"Well . . . I should." I stood up, and he backed away a little more. "I don't take kindly to being violently assaulted when I'm on my way to a planet-saving mission." Pinning him with my stare this time, I stepped forward and straightened his flight suit. He flinched. "But I think you saw the error of your ways, and that's important. I don't think you'll do it again." The question of whether he might have done it before hung potently in the air between us. "But if I find out you have, I don't care what else they do to you. Even if they throw you into solitary confinement at the deepest level of Zartlegarn, I'm still going to come for you." I widened my eyes and gave him a slight nod, and he stumbled and ran back to his seat. I collapsed back in my own, completely exhausted.

Barple said nothing to him and gave no acknowledgement of what he'd clearly overheard. Maybe he was used to Trank's antics. Maybe he'd taken his own turn before. I didn't care, as long as neither of them did this to anyone else again. I was just glad Miriam was still sound asleep.

The fact I'd used my mind was obviously something his own was too feeble to work out, even after I'd reiterated what I was doing on this trip and how important it was. He'd probably work it out in time, but that was for the good. It meant he'd take my threat even more seriously.

CHAPTER 6

In the beautiful Camzhargi palace, Princess Jasmila was having her hair braided in front of the full-length gilt-edged mirror in her quarters. It was up for debate whether the word "beautiful" could still be applied, however, after a Tevlar rocket had blown a sizable hole in the wall downstairs and destroyed the room behind it with a devastating fireball. Jasmila had admirably shrugged it off and continued with her business. After all, it was only the library, and she'd never been one for reading. So, what if it contained priceless four-thousand-year-old scrolls detailing the Camzhargi's history on the planet? Everything had been digitized so it was easily accessible for those who were interested in that sort of thing. Provided they pay a two-hundred-dollar subscription fee, which she'd argued to her mother was a benefit that could help swell the coffers in these difficult times.

Her mother, who always thought she knew what was best for her. Who clung to tradition as if she was clinging to the edge of a cliff. Who thought that Jasmila entering into a sham of a marriage was magically going to make everything okay again. Of course, it wasn't as simple as that, was it?

She was reclining on the purple chaise longue now with a cup of chamomile tea while watching her daughter, although Jasmila thought "scrutinizing" would be a more appropriate word. The angle of the mirror did not quite permit her to see her mother, but she could still feel her eyes boring into her head.

"At least consider it," said the older woman. "The Narbrutsi household is prepared to offer a trial period of a month. Now of course, everyone's hoping it will be longer. It doesn't mean the attacks will stop. But the Narbrutsi will come down much harder on any perpetrators."

"At the moment they aren't coming down on them at all," said Jasmila. "I'm not an idiot, mother. Do you really think I'm going to get down on my knees and beg for mercy from these barbarians?"

Her mother clicked her tongue irritably. "You're lucky to still be standing on your feet. Our home happens to have a gaping hole in it in the room directly below them. We were just lucky that the blast narrowly missed a load-bearing wall."

"Yes, it is rather a bother, isn't it?" said Jasmila, absently picking a piece of lint off the front of her lilac and pink taffeta-and-ermine gown. "But you know we can't succumb to such tactics, mother. That would make us no better than them."

"Maybe you don't care about the lives of our citizens," said the queen. Jasmila felt the venom lacing every word, but she didn't flinch. She'd grown accustomed to it. "But it's our lives at stake here too. Doesn't that mean anything to you?"

Jasmila coughed daintily. "Honour means something to

me. Holding firm and true to what is right. I thought those were the values this family had always upheld. Of course, you married in, so perhaps I shouldn't expect you to share them."

"Is it not right to save the lives of thousands of people?" Her mother threw her hands in the air. "Never mind, I can tell I'm fighting a losing battle here. You know, he's not such a bad old twig, that fiancé of yours. I think you'll feel differently in a day or so."

Ignoring the question her mother had asked, Jasmila appraised her appearance and dismissed the attendant with a loud snap of her fingers. "Mother, he's an insufferably boring and pompous prig, not to mention a dishonourable scoundrel. And I'm not going to feel differently in the next day, or the next year, or the next lifetime. So unless you know something I don't . . ."

The queen smiled to herself. "You wouldn't like that, would you?"

▭

Waking with a start, I reoriented myself to my surroundings. A car. Traveling through lush, dark green forest. So, this was the surface of the planet Sintrago. It had a tropical vibe, in this part at least. In the trees, I could make out red-tailed rataks—monkey-like creatures with protruding bellies—and long-beaked kwanataa birds, although the sky was drab and grey. I knew that none of it was natural.

Fragments of the super-realistic dream I'd had filtered through my subconscious. A spoiled princess. Big on self-centeredness and sense of entitlement, to put it lightly. And this was the very one for whom I was supposed to be sorting out her nonstarter of an engagement to try to put an end to the soul-crushing slaughter here. Hmm, could be a tall order. At the minute, Jasmila seemed totally intractable and hell-bent on sticking to what she thought was right for her, shells to her own palace notwithstanding.

That was according to the dream, anyway. I didn't know whether to trust it, but this felt like more than a dream. It was hyperreal, like I was seeing things through the eyes of the princess. It didn't mean I suddenly had an incredible insight into her psyche, because there was clearly a lot going on there, but this definitely felt like a heads-up that might help during the mediation. A psychic episode? I'd never experienced anything like it with anyone I'd helped before. I'd wait to see if it happened again, but I was due to meet up with the not-so-happy couple the next day.

"Nice sleep? This is beautiful, isn't it?" I turned to Miriam, feeling bad that this was pretty much the first time during the whole journey we'd both been conscious at the same time. Mind you, it wasn't like we could really talk freely while we were under an escort. I was just glad we'd ditched Trank and Barple along with the shuttle and were back to the middle-aged model of guard for this leg of the trip. I hadn't told her about the incident with Trank and had no plans to. She'd just freak and insist we go home or something, and I had no intention of letting some flam-for-brains jock distract me from my mission here.

"It really is," she said. "I mean, I knew about it, you might see it on the news every now and then, but it's nothing like seeing it in real life."

"Totally. And you don't really see it that much. I mean, there's nothing majorly newsworthy about rataks." Sadly, the news seemed to focus pretty much solely on the inner-city violence. The rainforests had been planted centuries ago by the first colonizers to keep the planet oxidated, and although thankfully there was still a government department that kept them looked after, they kind of got taken for granted as just part of the background.

"At least we're both awake for a change to see them," she chuckled.

"Yeah." She thought the trip had been uneventful, but boy, did I have a lot to fill her in on when we got to where we were staying. Now definitely wasn't the time, with another pair of interchangeable goons listening in. But I was looking forward to telling her and getting her feedback. In a weird way, I was excited. For the last eleven years I'd thought my ability was about doing one thing, and although given the choice I'd always go for the door that led to *not* being violated intimately, it had shown me I was capable of much more. And the dream? So vivid, so real. Like most people I only knew vague details of this stuck-up princess, but here I seemed to be privy to her innermost thoughts. Where was that coming from?

We hit the suburbs and passed by more and more houses, and although they were still interspersed with a few thickets of trees, the greenery eventually petered out altogether. We were in the city now, and the cracked cement high rise blocks with their general atmosphere of decay stood in stark contrast to the lush jungle canopies we'd seen not long before. Greasy-looking gangs gathered on street corners, though I couldn't tell if they were Narbrutsi or Camzhargi.

Eventually we approached a grand limestone structure, all fancy columns, towers, and balconies, standing in stark contrast to the depressing architecture around it. The royal palace. I'd seen it on the news, of course, but another dead giveaway was the yawning hole in the ground floor that I knew about from my dream. No doubt that'd be picked up by the media soon, but I'd been allowed a sneak peek behind the façade.

The driver stopped in front of the grand wrought iron gates, and they swung open ponderously. No doubt that was done by face recognition or whatever, but wait—we were going straight in there?

"We're staying here?" I exclaimed as the car inched forward and the gates closed behind us.

"That's right," said the guy in the passenger seat, the first words he'd spoken since we were handed over to our final pair of minders. "The queen wants you to be easily accessible, so this is the best solution for us all. Also, this is a war zone. The safest place for you to be is behind the walls of the palace."

"Err, dude, I hate to be the one to point it out, but one of those walls has got a bit of an explosion-type hole in it."

"That is an anomaly," he said, sounding confident. "We have increased our security tenfold, and guards are patrolling the perimeter twenty-four seven. Something like this will not happen again. In addition, your room is right at the heart of the palace and is quite safe from any hypothetical attacks—although, of course, we expect none."

"Good to know. But what damage could an aerial bomb do? Are you patrolling the skies above the palace too?"

"Do you think the hoi polloi have access to space shuttles?"

It was a good point, and I didn't have an answer to it. It was a good use of the word "hoi polloi" too—many mistakenly used it to refer to the privileged classes when actually the opposite was meant. Still, I'd like to know we were staying somewhere safe no matter how luxuriously appointed.

"Okay, you've sold me. I don't know why, but I'm prepared to put my life in your hands. I guess we don't have a choice though. Miriam?"

She shrugged. "As long as there's security in place. It's probably safer than anywhere else at the moment, I mean, the fighting's everywhere."

"Yes, but hopefully not for much longer, once your friend here has completed her mission. Hmm?" He turned round in his seat and winked at me. In response I simply gazed back—I didn't take this lightly, it was going to be tougher than anything I'd ever done, and I didn't want anyone else to either.

While we were talking, the driver had taken us down a descending ramp at the side of the palace with heavy iron shutters at the bottom of the steep slope. He held out his palm to a reader mounted on a pole in front of the shutters and they rolled up, letting us pass through into a brightly lit underground holding pen. After rounding a few corners, we pulled into one of the bays—I wasn't sure if it was specially reserved for this car or what—and we all got out, except for the driver. He hadn't said a word the entire time, and he didn't say goodbye now. Presumably he was waiting to go off on another errand.

"So, what happens now?" I asked the other guy as we picked our way along the railed walkways of the holding pen.

"I will show you to your rooms. You have separate quarters, although you are both free to move between them as you wish. Nothing will happen until tomorrow, but the princess has requested an early meeting with you alone before the scheduled intercession with both her and her fiancé."

Wait, that didn't sound right. What did she hope to

achieve by meeting with me alone? If the strange dream was anything to go by, Princess Jasmila was a self-centred lunatic who was prepared to do anything to shirk this betrothal to the Narbrutsi prince. If she meant to talk me out of doing what I was there to do, she had another think coming. Still, maybe a one-on-one could be useful. I'd always assumed I needed both parties involved in a dispute to be in the same room to be able to go into their minds, but maybe I could do it with just one. The eerily intimate nature of the dream was showing me there might be more to my ability than I'd thought. Ever since I'd left the safe confines of my moon, all the time I was finding out more about it.

We came to a lift, which opened as soon as the guard hit the button. It travelled up seven floors, and when the doors opened again, we were met with a plush hallway that stood in stark contrast to the industrial grime of the holding pen. A red carpet had a recurring pattern of gold shields, and little alcoves between the doors held marble busts, I guessed of dead members of the household. Intricate diamond chandeliers flooded the space with light.

"Come, your rooms are this way," said the guard, striding ahead. We followed, trudging down the long corridor past so many rooms that I lost count. They weren't numbered, and I wondered how they remembered which was which. I felt like I was in one of those ancient cartoons where the same background repeats endlessly.

Eventually we stopped outside the umpteenth door. Like all the others, it had intricately carved woodwork showing leaves and cherubs and whatnot, flecked with gold that really made the 3D effect pop.

"Miss Spindelman, this will be your room, and Miss Ganzapoli, yours is right next door. You will have your meals delivered here. Lunch is due to be served shortly. I trust everything will be to your satisfaction." He opened the door and ushered me inside.

I stood there and didn't make a move to enter. "Wait, don't we get key cards? Do these doors lock?"

He gave an odd half-smile, lifting one corner of his mouth. "There is no need for that. You are perfectly safe thanks to our security team, which is on patrol at all hours."

I wanted to tell him I hadn't been safe on the flight from a member of his team who was supposed to be looking after us. It sure didn't feel good to me knowing anyone could enter the room at any time, but I supposed I could deal with them the same way I did Trank—hopefully. It was Miriam I was worried about.

"As long as your security team is trustworthy," I said, holding his gaze and noticing there was something mocking about his, although that was how they all looked—smug and superior. "Come on Miriam, let's settle in and then you can come round to mine in a minute." I went in without looking back at the guard.

Throwing my bag on the floor, I allowed myself to take in the visual feast that greeted me. The room was pretty much as I'd expected from what I'd seen of the palace so far, although I still had to grudgingly admire the magnificence of the upholstery and the various old-school vases and paintings. Was that an original Trinanga-Cibur, twenty-third-century Earth if my art lessons served me right? There was an ornate carved fireplace with more cherubim and seraphim action and a ginormous four-poster bed with tasteful silken drapes. Plenty of space, with a couple of those chaises longue to lounge about on. It was about five times the size of my living room at home, and that wasn't counting the bathroom. Yeah, not too shabby. No windows, which did kind of give it a "gilded cage" vibe, but like the guy said, we were better off in the middle of the palace. And he hadn't actually said we couldn't come and go from here as we pleased, although wandering the war-torn and gang-infested streets was quite a long way down my to-do list right now.

I heard the door creak open behind me. It was pretty loud, so as long as I was awake, I would definitely know if someone was trying to get in.

"Hey, I think your room is even more drassic than mine!" said Miriam, making her way in. "I don't have a fireplace like that. I know they said we get meals at certain times, but do you think we could like, order room service right now?" She giggled.

I grinned in return. "Yeah, I could really go a big bowl of mikanfruit ice cream about now. This trip has been stress to the max, and it's only just beginning." Inclining my head towards the chaises longue, I said, "Let's go and chill as much as we can, and I'll fill you in."

So, I told her about the degrading attack by Trank and how I'd been able to ward him off by going into his mind, then about the eerily vivid dream that seemed to be beamed straight from the head of Princess Jasmila. All of which pointed to sides of my ability that I'd never encountered or tapped into before.

"Man, I'm so sorry I was comatose on that flight," she said, lying on her side with one crooked arm holding up her head. "What sort of friend is that? I knew those guys were off, and him in particular. I'd have made sure he never thought about doing that to anyone else again."

I waved a hand. "It's fine, I don't think he will anyway. At least I hope not. After I used my power, it was like he didn't know what he was doing there or why he was basically on top of me. Physically repelling him wouldn't have worked, even with two against one—he was a big guy. It would have ended up worse for the both of us."

"So, if he doesn't know why he was there, then who's to say he's learned?" She frowned. "What's to stop him reverting to factory settings, if you like, and trying the same thing with the next girl who's unlucky enough to end up in a confined space with him?"

I sat up and ran my hands through my hair. "I hadn't thought of that. Okay, we definitely need to report him."

"It's leaving it to chance otherwise."

"You're right, and I should've thought about that. My interventions have always been a one-time deal anyway. There's nothing to stop those same two people disagreeing about the exact same thing in the future."

"It's beyond disrespectful and unacceptable in any case, but when you're being brought here to try and resolve this whole thing . . ." She shook her head. "Okay, so what about the dream thing? What does that mean?"

"I don't know, but it was like more than a dream, the best I could describe it would be as a vision. I wasn't just dreaming about Princess Jasmila, it's like I *was* her. There's details I wouldn't have known otherwise. It was just so weird."

"Are you going to tell her?"

"I don't know. She wants to meet with me alone tomorrow morning before the intervention with her and the prince. I'm still not totally sure why. I mean it's not like I know what she's thinking right now or have access to her entire memory bank, it was just for those few minutes of the dream. I'm going to see what she has to say first. Right now, I can't see what difference it makes whether she knows I had this dream."

"Right. Well, it might help you get into her mind . . ."

I looked around the ornately appointed room, seeing things but not really registering them. "I know, but I need to get into the prince's mind too. And if I have this strong psychic connection with her, for whatever reason, then it might make it harder to strike a balance between the two. I don't know. I'll just need to wait and see."

She smirked. "Maybe you should request a private audience with the prince too."

Offering a goofy grin in return, I said, "I think a lot of people would be interested in that. Except our precious Princess Jasmila, apparently. I don't know what the deal is with that."

"Doesn't like being told what to do?"

I nodded heavily. "Yeah. She's been totally entitled and pampered her whole life, her every whim catered to. And then to be forced into something she doesn't want . . . I can't say I agree with her, but I can see where she's coming from."

"I can too, but it's the bit about disregarding the lives of millions that's hard to swallow."

"Definitely leaves a sour taste, and points to a lack of conscience. And the stronger minded someone is, the harder it is to work with them and break that down. And this chick's got a will of iron, it's so strong you could make girders out of it." I could almost feel my brain ache and the bile rise in my stomach as I contemplated mounting an intervention between the two meant-to-be-betrothed royals.

"Well, we'll see what happens at this meeting. Maybe you'll find out something you can use."

"I hope so." I yawned, stretching my arms over my head as I lay on the beguilingly comfortable chaise longue. "Man, I'm pooped all of a sudden. That was a really early start and a totally stressful journey, and I feel like it's all catching up to me. We should take the rest of the day to just kick back."

So, we did that, making the most of the free time to eat, watch movies, chat, and generally zone out. I could almost understand the thinking of those who were privileged and sheltered from all the deprivations outside—except in this case there'd been a breach to the defences, although weirdly even that didn't seem to worry Princess Jasmila. Despite the unexpected chance to have a girly catch-up day with Miriam, I couldn't quite get away from the looming task ahead of me. I'd never intervened in a dispute involving an arranged marriage, and it was a big ask to get two people to agree to enter into it if at least one was strongly opposed. It would be getting Jasmila to make that sacrifice for the greater good when she didn't even seem to care about her people. So, what would be in it for her? Maybe that would be what I had to get out of this meeting tomorrow. I didn't really know where the prince stood on things. He was an unknown quantity, and that worried me too. Jasmila was beautiful, sure, but if he knew the first thing about her personality I wouldn't be at all surprised if he was dragging his feet.

At the end of the night, Miriam went back to her own room, and I was left with my own thoughts. I wasn't any closer to a resolution, but I tried to tell myself to just see what tomorrow would bring, and then I pretty much blacked out from exhaustion.

CHAPTER 7

Jasmila sat in the antique wooden chair and painstakingly applied her makeup in the huge mirror overlooking the dressing table. She had a love-hate relationship with that chair. Yes, it was beautifully and intricately carved, but there were a lot of hard edges that didn't make it very suitable for certain, as it were, key purposes. At least the seat was upholstered in purple velvet.

The princess applied the finishing touches to her eyeshadow and appraised her handiwork. The galaxies forbid she would be seen by anyone without her full face on, and this wasn't just anyone. Despite being told her whole life that she was beautiful, a rare jewel, a prize—yada, yada, yada—Jasmila had always thought she was too plain to be a princess, and so her face, as she called it, was certainly not just cosmetic. She never let even the lowliest servant see her without it. And Nathaniel might be technically a servant, but he was far from lowly. He served her needs pretty well.

There was a knock, although it didn't come from the door. It had a distinct stony, echoey vibe to it. Jasmila stood up and adjusted her nightgown carefully before stepping across to the vast bookcase taking up one wall of the room. She'd never been a reader. Like the chair, like the mirror, like the bed, everything in here was inherited from her ancestors, like she had to live in some musty, old time-capsule. If it was up to her, she'd have sold it all long ago to buy more dresses, and she'd seriously thought about it on many occasions. But her mother was so freakishly attached to all this stuff that she'd probably have gone into meltdown and thrown her out of the palace, and then what would have become of her? It wasn't like she could get by on her looks if she didn't have access to her beautification aids. The outside was a wilderness of death, violence, gangs, scumbags and, worst of all, absolutely no servants. She shuddered.

After finding the right shelf, she stood at the bookcase and pulled out a slim dark blue volume. She lay it on its side and, moving to the left slightly, her hand went down to the shelf below and found a slightly bigger faded red volume. Finally, she went to the very top shelf with the help of a ladder on a thin rail that she wheeled across from the other end of the bookcase. A third book was laid flat on the bookcase, and she hopped smartly down, shoving the ladder out of the way as the section swung soundlessly outwards.

If someone was browsing here—though she didn't know who that might be—they might well go to the wrong book and have a look at it. Then pulling out the second book was that much less likely. If you added a third book into the mix, you started getting into million-to-one odds, and Jasmila was someone who didn't like taking chances. She'd had a carpenter install the three-book system in exchange for a ridiculously high payment.

"Yoo-hoo," she called as quietly as she could into the

dark opening that appeared before her. "Out you come." Clearly she wasn't one for scurrying through damp and dusty tunnels. He really was dense if he had to be reminded of that every time, but then it wasn't his mind that she was interested in.

A door opened and shut at the other end of the tunnel. The space opened to a clerk's office at the other end after travelling the length of the intervening room. Because that one wasn't used, people hadn't noticed that its dimensions had been reduced somewhat to make way for the enclosed passage. Yes, there were risks involved, but what was life without them? Sitting around waiting for an arranged marriage before popping out progeny to make sure she carried on this pathetic family line?

No, thanks.

Nathaniel emerged into her quarters; his pristine white shirt slightly dirtied from the tunnel. That only made him more alluring to her. Without a word, she grabbed him by the collar, threw him against the wall and kissed him roughly.

Jasmila liked being in charge of this . . . whatever *this* was. Certainly not a relationship. That would be anathema. But she couldn't guarantee she'd have control with that prissy prince.

Afterwards, as they lay entwined on the luxuriously appointed bed, she said, "I do enjoy our meetings, Nat."

He grinned and pulled a strand of brown hair away from her eyes. "As do I, and I'm happy to be of service for as long as you require."

Her focus softened slightly, and she looked away demurely. "You know it'll be much more difficult if they make an honest woman of me. Not that it would work.

Marriage would be a terrible inconvenience, and that's why I'm doing everything in my power to stop it."

"I don't doubt your capability in that regard. But there's rumours going around about some intervention they're mounting . . . a young girl who's able to do mind control or some such?"

She made a "tsh" sound and rolled her eyes. "Let them try. If they think I'm going to be brainwashed into an unhappy union, they don't know Princess Jasmila. But don't worry, I'm on the case. It's why I wanted to see you tonight —well, apart from the obvious—to tell you not to worry about it. I've requested a meeting with the little upstart ahead of the big showdown, or whatever you want to call it. I'm going to make sure that big get-together never happens —or at the very least, not in the way they hope it will."

He grinned. "You're a little genius. What are you going to do? Intimidation, bribe?"

"Something deeper than that. After this, she's not going to be invading anyone else's mind, believe me."

I woke with a start. A nightmare? If only. The details told me I'd once again had direct access to Jasmila's . . . well, her life, basically. I just wish it didn't include the more sordid parts. And I'd woken just before finding out what she was going to do to . . . what? Incapacitate me?

Bring it on, sister.

I may have woken at the wrong time, but I was going to be ready for Princess Jasmila. I don't think she knew about this sort of psychic link between us. Or maybe she did, and that's how she thought she could work against me. The idea that she was having the same sorts of dreams I had—seeing things through my eyes—made me want to pull off my own skin in discomfort.

After calming down and thinking things through a little

longer, it occurred to me that this might be the first time I had encountered someone with similar powers to mine. I'd never known whether others might be out there. But if she did, she certainly wouldn't be using them for the greater good—more likely this was how she managed to get her own way. Clearly it didn't always work, but her talk of disabling my powers or discouraging me from using them was a direct threat, and I certainly wasn't going to underestimate what she might be capable of.

What time was it? I checked my readout. Yeesh, 12:43. I needed to get back to sleep, but I didn't want to be privy to any more of Jasmila's late-night trysts. I didn't need the gory details. I lay there a while longer, thinking about what tomorrow might bring, and eventually drifted back to sleep —and when I woke again, I had no memories of any dreams or visions, which was becoming a blessing these days.

It was past seven now. I felt decently rested, which was just as well, because I was certain the day ahead would be taxing. I could happily have lay there longer in the supremely comfortable cocoon that was my bed, but I hadn't been given a time for when Jasmila would be visiting, and I had to prepare.

I got up, made the bed, showered, and dressed. It wasn't like I'd brought anything fancy to wear, but I tried to smooth out the creases in my navy blue miflon suit as best I could. No makeup either—I didn't need a layer of disguise to face the world like Jasmila—but I brushed my long hair and pulled it back in a neat ponytail. At nine, there came a sharp rap on the door. I took a last look at myself in the mirror over the fireplace and, satisfied, pulled open the door.

An elderly butler-type dude in a black suit that had seen better days stood there holding a silver platter with one of those cloche things on top. "Your breakfast, miss," he croaked.

Oh yeah, food. That was a thing. I hurried to relieve him of the tray, which was shaking slightly, and said, "Thank you." He nodded without saying another word, turned to the side and made off down the corridor with a somewhat crab-like gait.

Where was Miriam's? Maybe he was coming back with it.

The breakfast was delicious and old-school, like the dinner—eggs benedict, grilled sausage, bacon that was perfectly done—but I didn't really taste it, knowing Jasmila could show up any time. Given this mysterious link we seemed to have, I wondered if I would sense her coming. I messaged Miriam to ask if she'd got her breakfast and then sat on the chaise longue and waited.

Just after ten, there was a knock on the door that seemed much firmer and more decisive than the one the butler had given. That was her, I was sure of it. I'd already learned that for a princess, she didn't seem to be dainty or delicate at all.

My suspicions were also confirmed by the fact that, as I made my way to the door, I felt this wave of energy—psychic energy—that almost forced me backwards. It was like a force of nature, which was what Jasmila was, I guessed.

I opened the door to a vision of regal superiority. Literally—she was at least a head taller than me and only gave me the most cursory glance, which seemed to be mostly through her nostrils as her head was tilted back, before sweeping past me without a word and settling herself in one of the chaises longue, bolt upright.

I was left floundering at the open door, which I shut

before turning to face her. I didn't know what the protocol was, how I was meant to address this woman. Mind you, the princess didn't seem to follow any rules of etiquette and was basically a law unto herself, so what hope was there for me?

Moving across the room to the other seat as calmly as I could, I sat down and was about to open my mouth when Jasmila stopped me in my tracks. She meant business, clearly, as her outfit reflected—no longer dressed in a lavish ballgown but in a rather severely tailored suit in a deep fiery red. "I know who you are and why you're here," she said, sounding like the words were burning her mouth. "And I can tell you now, it's not going to work. I can get my staff to escort you back to the spaceport right now, it'll save us all time. No one, and I mean no one, tells Jasmila Camzhargi what to do."

I tried to reply, but forming words and sentences felt like too much for my brain to handle. What was going on? It was like I didn't just hear her words but felt them booming inside my head, drowning out all my own thoughts.

She continued. "We'll go to this . . . summit, this intervention, whatever you want to call it, for the look of the thing, of course. Appearances are very important to me, you know. But it will be a farce, a charade. You'll try your little mind tricks, as much as you want, but you won't break down my defences. I am stronger than you and stronger than anyone you've ever met. Then everyone will shrug, act all sheepish and apologetic, and send you on your merry way. And everything will carry on just the same as before."

Before? That wasn't good, was it? I knew it wasn't, but why? My thinking was slowing down, it was like my brain was going into a deep freeze that paralyzed its functions. I had to fight back. I had to stop listening to her words, but it was more than that. Whatever she was doing, it felt like a vine was wrapping itself around my thought processes and squeezing the life out of them. I gasped and nearly slumped over in my seat.

Seeing this, the princess seemed to get excited, her eyes widening, but she didn't cease her poisonous monologue, and then my vision swam out of focus. I had to stop looking at and listening to her. I had to try to tune her out and then hopefully her hold would be weakened. I was better than this bitch, I knew it, and I refused to let myself be broken by her. I tried going somewhere else in my mind, to when I was happy, me and Miriam sitting in my room talking about boys and all the usual stuff, not any of this flam. I would get back to that. I could sense Miriam through the wall in the next room, and that helped me. I tried to draw on the strength it gave me and let it be my anchor. Now, although I still felt the painful squeezing of Jasmila's talons, it was like I had more of a vantage point. I could get a handle on what she was doing and try to pry her loose.

But wait—was that the right thing to do? An instinct I couldn't really understand at first was telling me it was a bad idea—and then I knew why. Jasmila would sense I could fight her off and would redouble her grip, and worse— it would make the intervention harder. I would call her bluff. If she thought she had the upper hand, her defences would be down at the meeting, and then I could infiltrate and give her a taste of what she was giving me. She was strong, I certainly wasn't in any doubt about that, but I could handle it. Letting her keep thinking she was the stronger one was the best thing tactically for now.

Sensing my apparent submission, I felt her calling off her attack, and she smiled, although it was sickly and with her mouth only. "So, I think we understand each other," she said flatly. "I'll see you at the summit later, for what, I hope, will be the last time. Goodbye, Harica." She rose, smoothed down her outfit and made her way to the door. I tried not to look at her or make any response, acting like I was dazed and out of it. I mean, it wasn't too much of a stretch, she'd certainly given me a good pummelling. As soon as I heard the door close, I let myself collapse on the chaise longue and lay there to let my battered brain recover. When I began to feel normal again, I messaged Miriam to come over, and we discussed Jasmila's apparent tactics.

"So, basically, she's playing dirty ," said my best friend. "You want to play it super careful. You just don't know what she's going to do, and I wouldn't count on her letting her guard down at the meeting."

"I get what you're saying, but I'm counting on her thinking I'm not a threat. I haven't yet shown her what I'm fully capable of, and she's in for a shock, that's for sure. And I am stronger. I have to believe that, or I wouldn't be throwing myself in like this."

"Your self-belief is awesome," she said, one side of her mouth lifting in a half-smile. "But you don't know yet what *she's* capable of, and that could have been just a little taster she's given you. She could be preparing to totally wipe the floor with you later."

I gaped for a reply and pushed myself up from the seat, pacing across the floor and back. "I have to believe I'm stronger. This isn't like a physical battle where she could beat me through brute force. We're talking about the mind, and what I can do is only limited by what I think I can achieve—so this is all about attitude really. And the thing is, with her, she's small-minded really. It's all about what's in it for her, what she can get out of it. I'm about the bigger picture. I think with the right motivation on my side, and hopefully with my defences up, I'll come out on top."

I must have been coming across a bit shrill and aggressive because Miriam rose to intercept my pacing, planting her hands on my shoulders to stop me, make me listen. "Look, I'm sorry, I didn't mean to question your abilities. I know you've got this. It's just, you need to take all the possibilities into account, you know? Have your own game plan. Have options."

I nodded as I met her gaze. She was right, of course. I was so glad I'd brought Miriam along to keep me calm, keep me focused. She was grounding me, a reassuring presence in an environment where I felt totally out of my depth.

"And then, let's not forget about the prince. He's an unknown entity."

"Well, yeah." I pushed my hand through my hair, massaging my scalp. "But I get the impression, just based on what I've read so far, that he'll be just wanting to go along with it. For the greater good, you know?"

"A selfless act." She chuckled. "I mean, if he's going to marry someone like her, compliance would be the way to go, wouldn't it? It's pretty much self-sacrifice."

"Yeah." I started to giggle myself. Maybe I was delirious with the drama of everything that had already happened to me, but it felt good to loosen up, let off some steam. "I mean he's going to need a lot of luck—and is she going to keep this thing up with that court clerk? It'd be good if there was some other way to stop this ridiculous war than with this ridiculous wedding, but if it's what needs to happen, I'll do everything I can to do my bit."

"I think it will make a difference. We've done the history, back on Earth around the twentieth and twenty-first centuries a royal wedding really captured the public imagination."

"It did, yeah, until the whole thing collapsed—it was at

one of those weddings they were unmasked as a bunch of impostors with no royal blood at all, starting with Elizabeth II." I tsked. "That knocked public confidence a bit, but I get what you mean."

"Okay, so let's focus on what's next." She folded her arms across her chest and sat up a bit straighter on the chaise longue. "Are you ready for this meeting later on?"

"Yeah. I mean no." I cast my eyes around the room before settling them back on Miriam. "As I'll ever be, I guess. I'm just counting on the double bluff, hoping it'll be easier to get to Jasmila because she thinks she weakened me with her nonsense earlier."

And that was a leap I was going to have to take. I didn't actually know if it would be any easier at all.

"I wonder why she's got those powers," said Miriam after a few moments' silence. "You've never met anyone else who can do the sort of things you can do. For all we knew, you were a one-off."

I hadn't looked at it that way. I'd just been too shocked by her vicious attack, and then I was trying to figure out a way to use it against her. It was obviously out of the question to sit down and have a sisterly chat about her powers and where they came from, even if I'd wanted to. So, could there be more of us out there? Spread far and wide, maybe—there were a lot of other moons, other planets that had been colonized. And some might not even be aware they had the gift. It wouldn't do much good to dwell on it because I had no way of contacting these people or even knowing who they were.

All my energy and attention now had to be on the meeting at three o'clock. Definitely wouldn't be a good idea to underestimate Jasmila. Our conversation spun on into the afternoon, punctuated by lunch, though I found it hard to concentrate or taste it, and I tried really hard not to think about what happened to my stomach contents that time I had really exerted myself with Mrs Jangaman. The intervention I was facing was going to be like that but turbocharged.

CHAPTER 8

At about two thirty, a guard knocked on my door to escort me to the meeting. I asked if Miriam could come along for support, and he shrugged and said it was okay. It was the whole reason I'd wanted her along, after all, to be there for the difficult parts—just having her presence in the room would make a big difference, I hoped. We moved through the maze-like corridors and took a lift that seemed to be different from the one we'd come up in. I locked eyes with Miriam as we stood behind the guard, and she inclined her head and gave me a small smile. "You've got this," she was saying. I summoned up my own lukewarm smile even while my stomach was tying itself in knots.

The one thing I had going for me was that Jasmila already thought she had me beat after our little meeting earlier. That wasn't true. And hopefully, if she wasn't expecting it, I could ease my way into the cracks.

We exited the lift to a corridor that was much grander than the ones we'd seen so far, although that's not to say those could in any way be described as shabby. This must be the ground floor. Paintings seemed to cover every available surface and in every possible style—as well as classical vibes, there were modern pieces with bold lines and bright primary colours. To me it was like someone had thrown as many masterpieces as they could at the walls with no consideration for how they might go together, and I actually stopped looking as I felt myself getting sensory overload.

After a few twists and turns, which seemed inevitable for any journey in this place—I'd have a hell of a job finding the exit if I wanted to make an escape—we reached a particularly well-appointed set of double doors done in that fancy carved wood style with leaves, animals, even palaces. The guard pushed open one of the doors without knocking and motioned with his head for us to go through. After we'd passed, he shut it again behind himself.

I didn't have even a second to get my bearings before Jasmila rose from a large table in the middle of the room.."Ah, Miss Harica, how kind of you to join us. And early for our appointment, too."

I didn't say anything yet, holding her gaze for a beat or two, before I let my eyes take in the room. Early—I didn't even know what time it was, I was just here because the guard came to get me. She would know that. At the other end of the table was a man who must be the prince, although I couldn't see his face yet. And around the room on gold-upholstered chairs was a gang of onlookers, maybe fifty of them—a few guards but probably a lot of officials too, I guessed from both families, wanting to see if this precious union was going to come to fruition. My mind flipped back to my history lessons; crowds gathered in Rome to watch gladiators fight to the death. I was used to working with an audience of a few kids, but this was way too much. I didn't want to be watched being torn apart if it came to that.

"I want these people to leave," I said flatly.

"Not even a hello?" said Jasmila in a mock-offended tone. "A shame, I thought we might be friends. And these people are here to see that everything goes as it should. There's a lot riding on this meeting, as you well know."

"But your outcome is not the outcome that everyone else wants," I said, making no move to join her at the table yet.

"Perhaps they will learn that Princess Jasmila is not to be trifled with." She sounded mild-mannered when she said it, but I caught a glint of steel in her eye. I knew why these people were here—to see the princess being brought into line. She was like a wildcat who needed to be tamed and taken into captivity. It was just down to me to give them what they wanted. And yeah, I could sympathize with being forced into marriage against one's will, but unless a different way of stopping the violence could be found, this was the road ahead.

I didn't reply to her comment but moved towards the table, motioning with my head to Miriam for her to follow. I would need her beside me every step of the way. There were several chairs ranged along each side of the table, and Miriam and I sat down next to each other.

I glanced at the prince on my right. He was probably in his mid-twenties, I'd say, a bit younger than the princess, with brown hair brushed neatly back from his face and a well-trimmed beard. He had a kindly face, although he wasn't smiling—he looked like he was girding himself for an ordeal that lay ahead. If all went to plan, that would include a lifetime of married bliss with a scheming egomaniac. Just boply.

"Shall we begin?" I said. There was no sense in delaying the inevitable.

Jasmila waved a hand as though I'd casually asked if she wanted an afternoon tea. "I'm ready when you are."

I acknowledged her with the slightest incline of my head and turned to the prince. He hadn't said a word yet, and I wanted to make sure he was comfortable, or at least as much as he could be. "What about you, your . . . highness?" As I grasped for the appropriate title, I wasn't sure that was right, but I almost giggled out loud as it occurred to me I hadn't tried to address Jasmila in any such way.

The prince raised his shoulders just a little and offered me a thin smile. "I suppose. And please, call me Narbert."

"Okay." I felt a twinge of sympathy again. This mild-mannered prince was just trying to do his best for his people and manoeuvring him into a marriage with Jasmila was like throwing a lamb to the slaughter.

The princess snorted in a most unladylike way. "Can we get on with it? Some of us have eyebrow-bleaching appointments we don't want to miss."

I had to check myself before I said something undiplomatic. "It's important to make sure both parties are happy to proceed, otherwise the intervention won't work. So, if we're all ready, I'll ask you both to close your eyes . . ."

I heard a "harrumph" coming from Jasmila's direction but, glancing at her, I saw she did what she was asked anyway. After checking Narbert had done the same, I closed my own eyes. Obviously, she thought this was just a charade after the little intervention she'd mounted earlier. She was going to have to think again.

I tried to get a handle on the energy and the interplay between the two minds. Jasmila's was, as I'd expected, so much stronger, practically drowning out Narbert's signals by sheer force, but that didn't put me off. There would be something I could latch onto, a vulnerable side, even if it was buried extremely deep. Obviously, I would have to concentrate on Jasmila first. I gripped Miriam's hand for support.

The princess's complacency was what I was counting on. If she already thought she had me beat, hopefully her guard would be down.

Subtlety wouldn't be the watchword here. I didn't want to give her time to sense her own plan hadn't worked because then she would fight back all the more. I charged like a battering ram, launching a full-scale assault, but I quickly realized this wasn't going to work. Pulling off something like this was a delicate operation that needed the cooperation of both parties. The "bull in a china shop" approach wasn't going to cut it and wouldn't give me the precision required. Although there was a bit of give from Jasmila at first, once she rumbled my attack, her mind turned into a brick wall that I bounced off like a tennis ball. I tried to come back for more, attempting a more measured approach, looking for a crack somewhere, even a hairline one, but it was hopeless. It was like trying to tunnel under a mountain with my bare hands. Somewhere in the vicinity I sensed Narbert, bobbing haplessly about, buffeted by the slipstream caused by the battle between me and Jasmila. I couldn't help him. And we were both caught up in her orbit now, spinning helplessly.

I registered a yelp coming from the physical world and relaxed my grip on Miriam's hand. I must have had her in a vicelike death grip without even realizing it.

I tried to retreat but found I couldn't do it. I was a fly caught in Jasmila's web. The notion of failure—of letting people down, letting an entire *planet* down, causing untold numbers of further deaths—batted at me from somewhere at the back of my subconscious, but I couldn't give it my attention, it was white noise at this point. My survival instinct had kicked in and I had to get out, but Jasmila had me ensnared. I'd never encountered a mind as strong as this.

I couldn't even sense Narbert anymore. She wasn't interested in him—all her venom was reserved for me. In any other circumstance, I'd have hoped he could get as far away from her as he possibly could, both mentally and physically. But it seemed that wasn't how politics worked.

Trying not to panic, I looked for any sort of give or traction I could to get away myself, but there was none. A rush of endorphins kicked in and I felt like I was going to puke—*not again*—but this time it would need to be right here on the table. Physically I was rooted to the spot.

I couldn't think. Couldn't plot. My mind became an abstract concept, and I felt like I was floating, a tiny thought bobbing helplessly in infinity.

Then—nothing. Just nothing.

CHAPTER 9

I couldn't say that everything went black. Or that everything went white. Those are both colours, and therefore they're *something*. This was a total mass of absence, an aching emptiness, a void so all-consuming I couldn't even register my own existence. I couldn't tell where I ended and the void began.

I don't know how long I was there for, either. Not even time can escape a black hole.

Eventually, somehow, I became aware of myself again. Two arms, two legs, a head. I had a body, and I was bizarrely grateful for it. I wasn't in the void anymore, or at least not in such a bleak, hopeless version of it. But neither was I in the conference room, or whatever it was, or my room upstairs, or even my room back home. This new space *was* all white, with no discernible floor or ceiling or walls. But there *were* voices. I wasn't alone. When I tried to turn towards them, however, they receded. I saw no one, and I couldn't pick out anything they said.

I stayed very still in the hope they would come to me. Maybe they could help me get out of here.

". . . only here for a short time, I think. We'll see how we can help her." A woman's voice. It seemed to be getting closer again. I held my breath, although I wasn't sure whether I actually needed breath in this place, whether my bodily functions were just a reassuring approximation based on memory, whether I was alive or dead. A second voice joined in—a man, older, I thought, with a deep, rich timbre.

"They seem so few and far between now. So rare among the young. We should try to learn all we can about her power. It could be vastly different from ours."

I tried not to squeal with excitement. So, this place was a repository—some sort of heaven, maybe—for those who shared my power? Or at least something similar? I knew about Jasmila, of course, but it didn't seem like she planned on doing anything beneficial with her mojo, and I wasn't in a position where I could sit down and talk to her about it. I had to thank her for sending me to this place, though, even if it was unwittingly.

I risked a glance to my right, the direction I thought the voices were coming from, terrified they and their owners would disappear again. To my relief I saw a woman and a man coming towards me, both of an advanced age, although I'd say the woman was older, in that slightly hunched, shrunken way you get—

The man. I clapped my hand over my mouth to stop a gasp escaping my lips. My mind zapped back to the afternoon Miriam and I had researched the victims of the Carbrutzi ambush. Mauritz!

Before I could process it any further, they were in front of me with warm smiles, benevolence seeming to beam out of every pore. In real life, or whatever *this* was, I was struck by Mauritz's resemblance to Dad—the same smile and eyes, but his face seemed softer, obviously more lived-in, with laughter lines that showed he probably didn't take anything too seriously. The woman was short, only about five two, with grey hair cut close to her head and quick, bird-like movements. She'd obviously kept herself in good shape while she was alive—assuming she was dead. *I* wasn't, was I? I knew Mauritz was, so all bets were off at this point.

"Hello, dear," she said with a small, kindly smile playing on her lips. "It's so nice of you to join us. My name is Kinfala, and this is Mauritz."

Gratified my hunch had been right and it wasn't some lookalike, I cleared my throat, but when I tried to speak, my voice still sounded squeaky. "I don't think I had much choice. One minute I was in the Camzhargi palace, trying to grapple with that maniac's mind, then I was just—nowhere. And then here, but I don't know where *here* is, either."

Kinfala nodded, her round blue eyes never leaving my face. They were like pools of deep wisdom. "This place isn't really anywhere, in a physical sense, that is. It's where those who share our gift can find each other, and I'm sure you will learn much here. Your mind encountered a formidable foe, one that could have broken you, and it went into self-preservation mode. You're perfectly safe here."

I nodded, trying to absorb all this, knowing I had so many questions but struggling to grasp them. Mauritz hadn't spoken yet. I wanted to ask about my parents and why they went cold at the mention of his name.

It seemed best to get the most pressing question out of the way first, though. "Am I dead?"

Kinfala's eyebrows shot up, and she made a clucking noise with her tongue. "Oh, bless you, dear. No, you're not, though some of us here are. Your body—well, let's say it's gone on standby mode. Shutting down all nonessential functions so your heart and brain can keep going. If you've been taking care of yourself and eating well, you'll be able to stay like this for up to five days, letting your mind recuperate. In the meantime, we're happy to try and answer any questions. I'm sure you've got lots of them."

"Um, yeah."

It seemed I had trouble picking which one to land on out of the many that were flashing before me.

"It's no rush, there's no pressure here." It was Mauritz who spoke this time, his voice a deep rumbling baritone, warm and reassuring. And when he looked into my eyes, his own dark brown ones displayed a glimmer of recognition. If we all shared this gift, wouldn't he already know who I was? And if so, why hadn't he shown his hand yet? He was the one I had a lot of questions for.

"You haven't been here long, have you?" I blurted out.

Kinfala looked at him with a faint smile on her lips. "Uh, no," he said haltingly, the benevolent exterior wavering. "Just a couple of weeks."

"A victim of one of those senseless acts of terrorism you were sent here to try and stop," said Kinfala, compassion lining every syllable.

"I know. He's what made my mind up to do it. If the timing had been different, perhaps I could have prevented it. Because we're family, aren't we?"

His shoulders sagged slightly. "I wasn't sure if you would know me, but you seem highly perceptive in your abilities. I was worried you would hate me."

I studied this kindly, bushy-bearded old man, apparently overcome with guilt and remorse, and gave a lopsided smile. "You don't seem like a very hateable person. And the name Spindelman in the media reports was kind of a clue—it's not exactly a common name. I didn't have any evidence we were related. I didn't pick up any cosmic vibes from you, and I didn't know I might be able to commune with the dead. Up to now, I always thought I had to be in the same room as someone to get into their mind."

Kinfala reached out and touched my arm. "There's so much about your gift you've yet to explore, and we can help you do that. You might even have abilities that we know nothing of. You're young and full of vitality."

"Unlike me," said Mauritz, deftly not including the woman in his summation. "My own gift has been dormant so long. After—" He faltered.

"It's okay," I said. "I need to know how we're linked. I—I promise I won't hate you. But I need to know why my parents shut down at the mention of your name."

"I don't blame them," he said, nodding ferociously. "That's completely understandable." Letting out a heavy sigh, he went on, "I can tell you—or, maybe, I can show you."

"Show me—like with Princess Jasmila?"

"What do you mean?" said Kinfala, frowning.

"I've been having visions, seeing things through her eyes. It's how I knew she had no intentions of going ahead with this marriage. And obviously, when it came to the intervention between her and the prince, it was like trying to move a boulder with my bare hands—that's how I ended up here."

Kinfala clapped her hands and practically did a little dance on the spot. "But this is very useful! Your mission failed this time, but you will get another chance. And perhaps you can manipulate her. Being privy to her thoughts and emotions means there must be some psychic link between you two."

I hopped from one foot to the other in impatience,

struggling to make sense of it all. "What are you trying to say? Am I royalty?"

She smiled indulgently. "Perhaps not. Unless there was some line that branched off a long time ago . . . But you can be linked to someone without necessarily being related to them."

I put that idea to the side for later exploration. I needed to focus on one thing at a time, and there was something else she said. "You said I had access to her thoughts and emotions. I told you, it's not like that, I don't feel what she's feeling, it's just like I'm in the room, hovering. I need to be in the same room as someone to actually get into their head."

"All a matter of training. We can help you develop your abilities. If all goes well, you should be able to subtly shift her line of thinking without her realizing it, and that will be of great help in your plan."

Mauritz held up a hand. "I don't know if I'll be of much use in the training, sadly. My own powers have gone unused for so long."

Kinfala turned to him. "You just need to embrace them again. Everything is at your disposal."

"Hey," I said to him, "you were going to show me what our connection was. Can we get back to that?"

"Of course," he nodded. "We're getting ahead of ourselves. Let's focus on one thing at a time."

"Sounds good to me." I felt like I was suffering from information overload.

"OK, so just . . . concentrate on my mind. Block out everything else."

I knew how to do that; I didn't need him telling me. Still, he meant well, so I kept quiet.

Searching for his mind, I found it to be very pliable and

welcoming, apparently holding no ill will or malice whatsoever. What could he have done that caused my parents to react to his name the way they did?

I was about to find out. In front of me was a young Mauritz, obviously unfettered by age but recognizable from the twinkle in his eye. I'd place him in his early to mid-twenties. He was seated at a table with two other men of a similar age, one of whom he closely resembled. Another relative? They looked like they were brothers, and at a guess I'd place Mauritz as the older one, maybe by a couple of years. The other guy was starkly different in appearance, with short jet-black hair slicked back from his face, a sharp nose, and a generally shrewd and calculating look about him. The brothers, if that's what they were, looked much more amiable, with their mops of curly brown hair and soft features.

"That's me on the right." I heard Mauritz's voice, like a narrator on a streaming show. "Sitting next to me is my brother, Grame—that's your grandfather. I'm your great-uncle, by the way. And the other man is Grame's friend, Harlow. Let's listen in."

O-kay . . . I'd have to process these details later. I knew next to nothing about my grandfather and didn't know of Mauritz's existence until I'd seen his name in the news. I tried to focus on what the men were saying.

". . . can help you two," Mauritz was saying. "I know it sounds invasive, and I know you don't think it'll work. But it'll resolve this thing for you, I promise."

"Really?" said Grame. "You haven't done this since school. This is serious business we're talking about here, not a piece of stolen homework. You need to let us sort this out the proper way, like men."

"But that hasn't worked out so far, has it?" said Mauritz,

lifting his hands and smiling gently. "Just let me try it one time. If it doesn't work out, at least we can say we tried."

Harlow let out a dismissive "tschh" kind of noise. "Yeah, whatever. As long as we agree on *my* way, which is obviously the right one!" His tone was sharp and nasal, reflecting his somewhat oily appearance. I was reminded of a rat.

"Grame?" said Mauritz, gesturing at Harlow and shifting his eyes to his brother.

Grame threw his hands up, before slamming them back down on the table. "Alright, alright. Just one time. Let's get this charade over with."

"Come now, have I ever failed before?"

Neither replied, although Grame rolled his eyes. They sat waiting for instructions.

I understood the cynicism, I'd faced it myself. Whatever was at stake here, I knew Mauritz wouldn't have had an easy task on his hands. Adults' minds were so much harder to work with than kids. When you were a kid, your personality was still taking shape, your thoughts and feelings could be changed more easily. Adults were pretty much set in their ways, and their cerebral matter was much more unyielding.

"Okay now, so just . . . relax as much as you can. It helps if you close your eyes, just concentrate on breathing in . . . and out again."

They did as they were bid, and Mauritz started the intervention. I felt a powerful connection to the events. Even though this was something that had happened years before I was born, I felt like I was right there in the thick of it.

It became obvious quickly that Mauritz wasn't gaining much traction. While his brother's mind seemed pretty pliable and easy to work with, Harlow's reminded me of Jasmila's—monolithic and unyielding. Trying to change Jasmila's was like trying to flip a house over with a ruler. What was remarkable was that no one would suspect anything like that. I'd never seen an intervention from the outside while simultaneously being right in the middle of it, and anyone looking on would just have seen three men with their eyes shut, possibly engaged in meditation. The slight throbbing of a vein at Mauritz's temple was the only giveaway to his efforts if you were looking for it.

That all changed after a few minutes, though. It seemed like Mauritz had gained some ground with locating where the two friends were locking horns and was applying a lot of pressure. He'd got his shoulder up against that boulder—assuming someone could shift one in real life—and was pushing unrelentingly. If he eased off, he'd lose what little ground he'd gained and would have to start again. But because this was a three-way thing, Grame took some of the brunt of that pressure too, and his brain was straining under it. Back outside their heads, he clutched his fingers to his skull and started grunting and groaning in pain. Mauritz didn't seem aware of this at first.

"Stop!" I yelled, biting my lip in frustration. "Stop!"

But that was no good, of course. I wasn't there, I was a ghost, a wisp, a pulse of consciousness passing through the ether. I was powerless to stop the events unfolding in front of me. Of course, they'd already happened.

"I think that's enough," I heard Mauritz say. It was the older Mauritz, the current one—the *dead* one, I reminded myself. His voice roughened and deepened by age. I felt myself coming back to the moment like I was drifting upwards from the bottom of a deep swimming pool.

I slowly refocused on the two faces in front of me. It was

strange to see the face of the older Mauritz having just seen his younger counterpart in crystal clear vision—there must have been what, sixty years between them? "That was horrific," I said, shaking my head to try to rid it of the image of Grame engulfed in pain. I didn't want to ask what happened next—whether Mauritz had stopped. Didn't want to know. But I knew he would tell me, and deep down, I *had* to know.

"Grame died," said Mauritz, the words sounding distant. "They ruled a brain haemorrhage. I thought I was making some progress with Harlow and just kept pushing. I didn't realize that Grame was caught in the crossfire and couldn't take the pressure."

The voices of my parents started ringing in my head, all the times they'd chastised me for using my ability. I couldn't blame them. If it was me, I'd have forbidden it completely. Of course, I knew my grandfather had died. But the exact circumstances had been vague.

It seemed that Mauritz was waiting for me to say something, but I was still struggling to process. So, he went on: "Your father was only a baby at the time, and your grandmother was left to bring him up alone, a grieving widow. We never spoke again after that. I left to move planetside and never even contemplated using my gift again. I suppose I could have thought it through, understood it was a terrible accident, even considered using the power again in the right circumstances. But I just thought I was a monster. I was afraid of hurting those I loved or anyone else."

The guilt he must have dealt with was unimaginable. Also hard to understand was why my parents had let me use my gift at all, albeit grudgingly. Maybe they thought I wouldn't be able to live with myself if I'd known the circumstances of my grandfather's death. Maybe they thought dealing with kids' minds wouldn't be as harmful— but surely, they were more vulnerable? They'd certainly been keen on stamping it out completely now that I was older.

"I'm so sorry," I said to fill the yawning silence that invaded the space when Mauritz stopped talking.

He waved a hand. "Don't worry. I have had more than sixty years to come to terms with it—I moved to the planet, started a different life. In fact, I hadn't thought about my power for a long time—that was until my own death a few weeks ago, when I came here. That's not to say I don't think about my brother. I carry him around in here" —he pointed to his heart— "and I grieve for the life he could have had. What he could have become. But the exact circumstances of his death? It's not something I dwell on. I suppose, for my own sanity, I subconsciously realized that it was just an accident."

"Of course it was!" I reached out to touch his arm, finding he had physical form rather than being an insubstantial ghost. I wanted to comfort him. He was a nice man who didn't deserve to be wiped from the family tree. "You were trying to do the right thing. To help people. If anything, it was Harlow's fault for being too stubborn."

He lifted his glasses with his finger to wipe away a tear that was forming. "No, it's not his fault. It's not anyone's fault. He was hot-headed, you could say . . . ambitious. I couldn't blame him for that."

"Amazing you could forgive him. I wonder what happened to him. Whether he thought he was to blame in any way."

He shrugged. "No way of knowing. He didn't say anything about his feelings on it before I left. In fact, I never spoke to him again after that night. He was Grame's friend . . . I don't know whether he blamed me. It doesn't do any good to fixate on these things."

I admired his attitude. Like he said, he'd had a long time to come to terms with it.

There was something off about the whole thing, though. "My parents didn't tell me anything. I knew my grandfather died when Dad was a baby. But I didn't know the details or anything about him. But why couldn't they just tell me everything? If this ability was so dangerous, I would never have used it at all. I don't want to end up killing someone without even realizing it."

Kinfala spoke again, taking me by surprise. "That would have scared you. I can understand where they were coming from. You would have seen it as a curse, and it would have dominated your life. Instead, they tried to contain it. As you said, it was harmless enough when you were dealing with just kids. Until that intervention between the two members of staff at your school took a toll on you. But they didn't tell you someone could have died, they told you it was having too big an impact on your own health, and it was too much of a distraction from your schoolwork."

I frowned at her, feeling somewhat invaded. "How do you know all this?"

She smiled, more with her eyes than her mouth. It was obvious to me this was a woman who didn't cover up her emotions. "I've been watching your progress with interest. Because of the potent nature of your gift, you shine out like a beacon. I've been up here for more than thirty years, and you were the first one with the power to come onto my radar. There are not many of us, and you are very special. Mauritz has helped me fill in the backstory. Because his power was dormant, I wasn't aware of him until he appeared here."

"Wait . . ." I wasn't totally comfortable with being watched and followed my entire life, but I shoved that to the side for now. "So, aren't there any others here?"

"Oh, yes. We can meet them anon if you wish. All have been here longer than me, some for hundreds of years. They keep to themselves a lot, although we meet and talk from time to time. Meditation is a big pastime here. I engage in it myself."

I looked around at the featureless expanse of white—slightly misty, slightly translucent, certainly no landmarks to be seen. "Doesn't it get boring?"

"My child," she laughed, "that is impossible when you are attuned to the thoughts of others. In fact, we spend a lot of time trying to drown out the noise. That's why meditation is so popular. Boredom is the aim."

"I don't have the thoughts of others constantly going through my mind," I said.

"Well, when you live with others who share the gift . . . the noise can be unbearable."

It made sense, although I hadn't noticed it up to now. Perhaps I'd been too preoccupied with trying to figure out where I was and what was going on. I shut my eyes and tried to tune in to what was around me. Soon I felt . . . little scraps of memories. Emotions—anger, happiness, guilt. Grudges long held that weighed down the mind. All melding into a wall of noise that would become maddening if I let it. Ugh. I opened my eyes and tried to shake it away, focusing back on the two people in front of me.

"Okay, I get it," I said. "I wouldn't want that mess filling up my head all the time. I mean, how would you sleep?"

Kinfala smiled. "We have no need for sleep here. Meditation can help us reach inner peace."

They could sign me up for inner peace just as fast as they liked, but it was nagging at me that I had to get back. To finish what I came here to do. Well, not here, but . . . there. "Sounds drassic. I'd love to learn about meditation, but I don't have time. I've got a job to finish back on the planet. I need to stop the war and stop people dying. Could you help me get back there?"

Her eyes crinkled around the edges as she frowned. "I'm afraid I can't help there. Your mind needs to recover. You're receiving medical attention, but they can't do anything for your mind . . . you have to let the process run its course."

I huffed. The fighting was still going on while I effectively lay in a coma. I couldn't tell if it was getting worse, or better, I wasn't good enough to tune into the minds of regular people without the gift who were on a different plane of existence. I didn't really want to meet the other people who lived here. Maybe another time . . . I had to get back. Maybe I could meditate my way out of it.

"My dear, meditation is a way to achieve spiritual harmony and balance." Of course, I didn't have to vocalize my thoughts . . . I felt oddly naked. "I do not know if it would help repair a mind that has been overly stretched and strained, but it would certainly do no harm. I can teach you if you like?"

I nodded. "Let's do it."

CHAPTER 10

My eyes shot open. It took a few seconds for them to focus, but I got an immediate impression of opulence and luxury that told me I was still in the palace, albeit an unfamiliar room. I was lying in an ultra-comfortable bed in some kind of silk nightgown, a tube in my arm pumping in fluid from a sleek metallic machine next to me. Apparently, this was what was keeping me alive. I had no idea how long I'd been out. It didn't feel like long at all that I'd been in the other plane, but maybe time passed differently there. I was alone.

Where was Miriam?

I struggled to sit up and cast my eyes around the room as if expecting to find her holding vigil in the corner. This wasn't right. I didn't expect the medical officials, or whoever, to be there all the time, but Miriam should be by my side, where else would she be? It was the two of us against the world. We didn't know anyone else down here.

I tried to tell myself to calm down. There'd be a reasonable explanation, like she'd just gone to find something to eat or to use the bathroom. I couldn't begrudge her those things. But I needed to know what was going on and when I could get back to the job I came here to do.

"Hello?"

My voice was croaky, like I hadn't used it for days. I doubted anyone would have heard me. It wasn't like a hospital where there'd be doctors walking up and down all the time. But that was bad—what if something terrible happened quickly? I looked for water on the bedside cabinet to quench my throat, but there was neither water nor cabinet. I cleared my throat as best I could and tried again.

"Is anyone there?"

Still sounding strangled, I fell back against the inviting pillows and let my eyelids flutter shut. Miriam would be back any time now, I was sure of it.

When I opened my eyes again, Princess Jasmila was standing over me, regarding me like a curious species of insect she was studying.

"Ah, she's back with us," she said in a voice like velvet. "I rushed to your side as soon as you were back in the land of living, but you dozed off again. Disappointing. I was so looking forward to us being able to talk again."

I gripped the mattress with my hands to try to pull myself into a sitting position. Of course, it made sense that the princess would know when I'd come round. I should have been prepared for that. I looked around the room, but there was no one else there I could see. "What's going on? Where's Miriam?"

"All in good time, my little one." She gave me a lopsided smile. "Rest assured your friend is in the best possible hands. You don't need to worry about a thing."

"What does that mean?" I met her gaze, seeing nothing but concern and compassion, but I knew it was a front. I tried to see into her mind, but her defences were up. "Have you done something to her? She's my best friend. We came here together, and she's here to support me. I don't know why she isn't here."

She sighed. "If you knew how to make the best use of your gift, you would know why she isn't. But I'm too good for you in that department. I'm going to have to just tell you instead, and I won't enjoy that."

Another lie. I knew it. "Tell me, you bitch," I said through gritted teeth, dreading the answer.

She put a hand to her chest and gasped. "I don't think there's any need for that. I saved your life. Making sure you get the best possible care while you're incapacitated, and that's the way you speak to me?"

"It's your fault I'm lying here. Get this thing out of my arm and let me get out of this bed."

"Easy, now. I couldn't have you up and about before you're back to full strength." She put a hand on my shoulder as if I was about to rip the tube out of my arm and leap out of bed. Although she wasn't applying much pressure, I sensed a formidable strength. I sighed and relaxed, and she took her hand away. Truth be told, I didn't feel up to making any sudden moves, but I hated the fact she'd put me in this position. I wouldn't be lying here any longer than I needed to.

And I needed to know where Miriam was.

"There are four hundred and twenty-seven empty rooms in this castle," she went on, as if reading my mind. What was I thinking? Of course she was. "My mother and I do not take up that much room, even with the servants. Those rooms in the remoter parts are very useful. Even if you could manage to find the right one, she would not be able to hear you knocking on the door or yelling, thanks to the soundproofing."

I gulped, my stomach recoiling at the creature in front of me, pulsing in my brain like a live current. Remind me again why I'd brought Miriam here? Now she'd ended up as collateral in some sort of sick flamming game played by a pampered psychopath . . . who'd just become my puppet master. As vile as it was, I was going to have to dance to her tune if I wanted to keep Miriam from harm.

I forced myself to stay calm, not wanting to show weakness by losing the plot. "Is she safe?"

Examining her perfectly lacquered nails with interest, she said casually, "Oh yes, perfectly so . . . She has three meals a day as well as entertainment. But if you should do anything stupid . . . like, I don't know, trying to get the better of me at the next scheduled farce of an *intervention* . . . well, then I can't be responsible for what happens to her."

"Of course you're bloody responsible," I ground out.

She carried on as if she didn't hear me. "Know this—I won't be told what to do, especially by some little upstart like you."

Then it hit me. I had an ace in the hole, why didn't I think of it before?

"Of course, I could tell everyone what happened to me in the space shuttle on the way down here."

"Hmm . . . really?" She narrowed her eyes, and I squirmed uncomfortably as I knew she was probing my memories. I wished she would keep out of my head. Then she actually laughed, and I felt an overwhelming urge to punch her teeth out. "Well, assuming this isn't some product of your deluded imagination, and assuming people would actually believe such a thing of our well-respected space fleet, what do you mean by 'everyone'? Or anyone?

You're incapacitated, sequestered in a soundless room somewhere in a vast palace, just like your friend. You don't get to outsmart me, so I'd rather you didn't bother."

I lay there unmoving, although every part of me was simmering—all I wanted to do was wrench myself out of bed, lay this bitch out and go and find Miriam, but where would that get me? In a worse position than where I was now. I just didn't want to show she was getting to me, although my efforts were probably futile when she seemed to get into my mind so easily.

Instead, I tried to get my bearings. I wanted to know where and when I was, although I didn't know if that would make any difference. "How long have I been out?"

She shuffled in her seat, pulling her shoulders back. "Oh, not that long. You've made a remarkable recovery, considering you tried to outdo me when I expressly told you not to. Five days."

I groaned inwardly. Our parents were going to be out of their minds by now. I'd have to try to message them.

"Well, if there's nothing else to say, I'll leave you to *recuperate*," she said, rolling her eyes as if I was an ineffectual weakling to have ended up in such a position. "The medics say the drip can come out tomorrow if all is well. The intervention is scheduled for the day after, although it will merely be for show, of course. Once you fail, your friend will be returned to your side and you can go back to your safe little life on that moon of yours. They're not going to try you a third time once they see you're completely useless. I think that sounds like the best outcome all round, don't you?"

I stayed silent, not wanting to dignify this creature with a response.

"Well, have it your way. I see you need to rest."

I kept looking up at the ceiling until I heard her footsteps recede and the door shut. Then I let my body relax, shutting my eyes and feeling the tingling in my nerves die down a bit. I didn't know what I was going to do, but I couldn't let things play out the way she wanted.

I went to activate my infochip to message my parents and get some updates on what had been going on the past few days, but when I waved the fingers of my right hand over my left palm, nothing happened. What the flam? I tried different movements and patterns, but nope—nada. It had been switched off somehow. I didn't even know that was possible.

Thanks to that scheming witch, I had no clue what was going on outside while I was in this soundproof bubble. Had there been more attacks, killings? Would the situation be exacerbated once word got out the intervention had failed? Had I only made things much worse by coming here?

Then it hit me. I wasn't just confined to this room. I had at least one vehicle that allowed me to see outside—Jasmila. I'd seen things through her eyes before, but it wasn't something I felt I'd been in control of, it had just happened. I still didn't know what the link between us was, other than that Jasmila was so strong, and her personality so big, that her mind acted as a beacon for anyone tuned into that mental plane. Whatever. If I could hitch a ride, she might just lead me to Miriam, although I had to remain undetected.

I lay on the bed, trying to slow my thoughts down, tuning into the general energy of the building around me. I didn't look for Jasmila in particular. That would be a mistake and would give me away for sure. However, it wasn't long before I found her, the pulsating rhythm of her presence a dead giveaway. She did nothing to hide it, her arrogance her downfall as she assumed herself to be unassailable, that I could do nothing from the confines of my room.

I found myself back where I was the first time I'd inadvertently tapped into her consciousness—in her room, looking at her in the mirror while she sat at the dresser and lazily brushed her hair. She'd been talking to her mother, the queen, on that occasion, but this time she was alone. Information about Miriam's whereabouts was not immediately at hand. I could have tried looking for it, but I didn't want to probe too deep or I'd surely be betraying myself. I had to maintain a light touch and ride this out for as long as I needed to.

Without going too deep into Jasmila's mind, it was hard to read what she was thinking from looking at her eyes in the mirror. They were very pretty, but ultimately blank. Like most sociopaths, did she lack empathy? How did the deaths of thousands of her population affect her, something she could help address if she stopped clinging bloody-mindedly to what she wanted?

I shuddered. I didn't really want to know, and it wouldn't help me.

The minutes dragged on. I didn't know how many exactly, but she'd finished brushing her hair, applied a subtle tone of lipstick, and was now simply staring at herself with the same blank expression. What was it like to be that self-absorbed, I wondered? I couldn't imagine spending hours on end just looking at myself. So many other things were far more interesting.

I hoped we were waiting for something, that I would get some clue to Miriam's situation soon. Then it occurred to me, what if she was off to meet her lover again? Getting all dolled up, although she wasn't in her nightdress this time. I had no interest in being a mental third wheel again, and if it came to that, I'd probably just get off the space shuttle and try again later.

An uncertain, but stultifying amount of time later, Jasmila got up and paced around the room for a few moments, before activating the triple-book-mechanism secret passage bookcase thing. This was where her lover had entered the last time, although there was no indication of his arrival, thank goodness. Instead, we were going in ourselves.

There was plenty of room in the passage, Jasmila being on the svelte side, although it was a bit dank and dusty. I could smell everything she smelled too, and I was kind of getting that musky scent of an underground cavern.

At the other end, we reached a blank wall, although I knew there would be more to it than that. Sure enough, Jasmila reached down and easily found some mechanism near the floor that allowed the wall to soundlessly swing open in front of her. She passed through, not turning around to let me see what was on the other side—probably another bookcase—but as soon as I clocked the occupant of the room, everything else went out of the window.

Miriam.

CHAPTER 11

She lounged on the bed, looking like she was in a half-dozing state. I wouldn't have been surprised if her chip had been deactivated too—it was amazing how conditioned we'd become to having some sort of device constantly to hand, literally, over the past few hundred years. At least she wasn't tied up or anything, but there was no need to do that, there was no way out of the room. Unless she somehow found the secret passage, but with it taking her directly to Jasmila's quarters, it wouldn't help her and would probably only see her movements restricted further.

She raised her head groggily and looked at Jasmila with flat eyes. Based on what the princess had told me, she'd effectively been in solitary confinement for five days. That was enough to start getting to someone. At least I'd had the privilege of being out of it while I was making new friends in the no man's land between dreaming and waking.

"Are you with us?" said Jasmila, as if chastising Miriam for not being as fresh as a daisy. "I thought you might like to know that your friend Harica has woken from her slumber."

Miriam took some time to focus on the woman. Then

she seemed to come to herself and shook her head, a bit of defiance entering her eyes. "Right, okay, so can she finally do what she came here to do? It's your fault she ended up in the state she did."

Jasmila giggled. "My dear, I'm afraid you're naïve if you think the task placed upon your precious Harica's shoulders is easy. If I was going to give her a free run, I might as well go ahead and marry that fool off my own back and save you both the trip."

Miriam's eyes narrowed. "You don't like making life easy for anyone, do you? Surely a princess should be public-minded, thinking of what's best for her people. If this marriage is like a magic bullet that'll resolve all this, shouldn't it be a no-brainer?"

"How little you know about decorum, about diplomacy. How should a princess act? Well, what would a silly child from a backwater moon know about that? I don't think I would be setting a very good example to my female subjects if I accepted any old husband that was foisted upon me."

"You can't set an example to anyone if they're dead." Miriam scoffed and shook her head.

"Young lady, you speak out of turn. I ought to have you—"

"What?" Miriam cut in. "What else can you do to me? You've already had me locked in here with no human contact for what—five, six days? And no chip, no one to talk to. Why? Do you think I'm in league with the protestors and the mobs out there? I don't know anyone here. I came to support Harica, and I haven't even been able to see her since she ended up in a coma. Maybe my voice, my presence, could have helped somehow."

I felt Jasmila smirk. "I think you underestimate what being in a coma means."

"Whatever. She's awake now, so can I go and see her? There's no need for any of this, is there?" Miriam gestured around her.

"If only it were that simple. But I fear you two might plot to escape. I haven't finished with Harica yet."

"What does that mean? We're not going anywhere, even though our parents are going to be worried sick by now. She'll finish doing what she came here to do."

I could feel the friction and the sparks between the two as they argued back and forth. While they continued, I tried to think. Was there a way I could reach Miriam somehow? Let her know I was here? Hitch a ride on some of that energy flowing between these two?

I had to concentrate. It wasn't going to be easy. Up to this point I'd managed to remain a spectral presence, basically sitting on Jasmila's shoulder but remaining out of her eyeline. The princess would need to be the conduit if I was going to get to Miriam, but I had to do it without Jasmila detecting me.

It looked like I was going to have to ramp up the heat somehow, then hopefully the mental noise of the argument would mean Jasmila wouldn't notice me leapfrogging her to get to my best friend. I wanted her to incapacitate the princess somehow and then come find me. It might be the only way. If I let things play out to get to the next intervention and I failed again—well, there wouldn't be another chance. Jasmila would get her own way, the war would continue, and my trip would have been entirely for nothing.

The princess seemed fairly in control. I had to try to amplify her anger a bit and get Miriam to react, maybe even scare her a bit. It wasn't something I wanted to do, but I couldn't really get a read on Miriam, and I had to heighten her senses. It would make it easier to speak to her.

The whole thing seemed counterintuitive because normally I was trying to defuse a conflict, not elevate it. But as I homed in on the point where Jasmila's and Miriam's minds were overlapping, I felt the thrumming tension and thought I could bring something to the party—my own sense of frustration at being unsuccessful at what I'd come here to do. I poured myself into the mix. Jasmila was so self-absorbed she wouldn't notice me—she'd feel herself getting angrier but wouldn't stop to think I could be behind it.

"The only thing that's going to be finished is your pathetic little friend," snarled the princess. "Finished on this planet, that is. There's no way I'm going to be humiliated and made to look weak by letting her win. Yes, we'll go through the motions again, but it'll be useless—I'll give her such a hard time that she'll never be able to use her pathetic powers again."

Over my dead body. A wave of anger flowed out of me inadvertently, but Jasmila was so riled up that she didn't notice. My anger fused with hers, and the momentum catapulted me towards Miriam, who was growing more defiant and showing her hand more in the fight.

"How can you be so cold?" she said, jumping off the bed and squaring up to the princess, although she was a good two inches shorter. *Yes, proximity was good.* Being physically closer to the vessel I was using did make it easier to get to her. "You're so determined you're not going to be told what to do, you end up looking like a monster because you care nothing for others. You're the one who's pathetic."

"You dare speak to me like that, you little worm?" spat Jasmila. "You have no idea what I'm capable of. Well, you're going to find out."

I didn't want to stick around for both me and Miriam to find out. I piggybacked on Jasmila's rage and threw some of my own in there to launch a shower of energy towards Miriam. She wouldn't exactly know why she was doing it, but she knew she had to overpower the princess and get out of that room—that was the mental impetus I directed at her. She lunged for a golden chair that was sitting at the foot of the bed and swung it at Jasmila's head. The princess was caught off guard and staggered, but soon righted herself and wrenched the chair out of Miriam's hand, despite a thin trickle of blood from a gash in her temple. Flam, she was made of stern stuff. She wrenched the chair out of Miriam's hands, grabbed her by the shoulders and spun her round, then twisted Miriam's right arm up behind her back, nails digging into her wrist. Being mentally invested in the whole fight, I could feel both of their pain, but Miriam's was worse. I guess that was indicative of the bond we had. I needed Miriam to get the upper hand again, so I summoned all my energy into a ball and unleashed it towards her consciousness—it was enough for Miriam to kick out backwards so her foot connected with Jasmila's stomach and winded her. The princess let go of Miriam's wrist and stumbled, and Miriam whirled around and launched an almighty headbutt that connected with her opponent's nose with a sickening crack.

That was the last thing I saw, however. Miriam must have hit her hard enough for her to lose consciousness, and that meant my ride with Jasmila had come to an end. Instantly I was back in the bed in the little room where I'd been laid up, feeling like I had whiplash. The last thing I'd seen was Miriam's face coming towards me—towards *Jasmila*—with a burning fury in her eyes like nothing I'd seen before. Wow, I was proud of my girl. She really came through for me. Although I was pulling the puppet strings, she took it somewhere I'd never expected.

I didn't know what would happen next, though. Hopefully Miriam was taking the opportunity to escape while Jasmila was incapacitated. It would be good if she could tie her up somehow. Despite the predicament we were still in, I couldn't help smiling at how Miriam had handled herself—I knew she was made of strong stuff, but that was totally badass! And Jasmila wouldn't be looking so pretty anymore . . . not that I was an advocate of violence, but she didn't seem to care about it happening to her own subjects, so it was poetic justice in a way.

The next issue was how me and Miriam were going to find each other. I had to assume she wouldn't be staying put —you wouldn't want to be there when Jasmila came round. I thought about coming for her myself, but we had a better chance of finding each other if one of us stayed where we were rather than both wandering round a maze-like palace. Now Miriam would be in a locked room just like me, but she also knew Jasmila had come in via another route. I had no idea if it was possible to get back through to Jasmila's quarters or what the mechanism was, but if it was similar to the one at the other end, there was no way she'd have time to try every single combination of books. No, her best bet was to get out the room the old-fashioned way, but without a keycard that was going to be difficult. Maybe Jasmila had one on her person? Or perhaps she could drag her over and see if her palm would work on the ID reader, but I didn't remember seeing if that door had one. Maybe she could try banging on the door and shouting for help, but the soundproofing meant that was probably in vain. Or she could try breaking the door down with a heavy object, if there was something like that lying around she could use. I went and checked out the door to my own room. It seemed pretty solid.

So many variables. I definitely wasn't in control now. All I could hope was that Miriam would use this opportunity to try to find me, but I didn't even know what we'd do if we succeeded—try to get away? No, I felt an obligation to the people here. The conflict had already affected my family—even if it was a family member I didn't get to know while he was alive, but I'd like to have had a chance to. I had to finish what I'd started.

I laid back on the bed and tried to sleep—I kind of hoped I could access the plane where I'd spoken to Mauritz and Kinfala. Maybe they could give me some advice. I didn't know if I could get to that place just by thinking about it or whether it happened at random or when I needed guidance, but I definitely needed it now. I didn't know how long Miriam would take to find me, I just hoped to God she made it out of that room before Jasmila came round. All bets were off if it came to that.

In the end, though, my mind was buzzing too much to get anywhere close to sleep. And I didn't have to wait too long as it turned out. Though I didn't have any way of telling the time, it couldn't have been more than half an hour before the intercom went at the door.

My stomach did a little flip as I jumped up to answer it, but then I thought—what if it wasn't Miriam? It could be one of the guards come to drag me away somewhere else or even a doctor or someone who was going to neuter my ability so I couldn't do any more damage. All of a sudden opening that door felt like lifting the lid on an unknown future that might just blow up and hit me in the face.

"Come on, open the door! Are you there?"

Miriam! I'd recognize those sweet tones anywhere, and

they never sounded more beautiful than right now. I rushed to the door.

Of course, it was locked, and I didn't have the credentials to open it with the reader. What was I thinking? I must have been really out of it. Jasmila was never going to just let me walk out of here any time.

"I can't open the door, it's locked," I yelled over the intercom.

"Okay, we'll get someone to open it." I didn't hear anything more for a few minutes after that, but I kept thinking, who was *we*?

When the door eventually opened, I did a double take and froze to the spot. It wasn't just Miriam standing there, but a man—the prince no less, the Narbrutsi prince who was supposed to be betrothed to Jasmila. There was another man walking away, a guard, who must have opened the door for them. I backed up a bit and then did a little curtsey, then felt like an idiot. I hadn't done anything like that with Jasmila, but then she didn't command my respect. This man seemed good and kind, with a twinkle in his eye. I got the same feeling of warmth I'd encountered during the intervention. I still didn't know him, though, and instinct told me to be wary.

"Harica! Thank goodness you're all right," said Miriam, bustling into the room, followed by the prince. I had to step out of the way. "I didn't know whether you'd be out of bed or not. I'll tell you how I escaped from my room, but it's kind of a long story—"

I put my hand up to stop her. "I know some of it. I've got a long story too, but I found out Jasmila has the same sort of power I do, but obviously doesn't use it for anything good. It means I can tap into her consciousness, see what she's seeing—"

"Wow! And she doesn't detect it?"

"I guess she's just too wrapped up in herself to notice. Or, you know, I'm just too good."

Miriam grinned. "Oh, hang on, I'm totally forgetting my manners. We'll come back to the princess in a minute, but this is Prince Narbert."

"Well yes, I know, we met at the intervention, although we've never actually spoken—Good afternoon, Your Majesty, I mean, uh—Your Highness." I gave myself a mental kick to stop rambling.

He waved a hand in a gesture that was both casual and somehow extremely regal. "Please, call me Narby." So, we'd moved on from Narbert. I liked him more all the time.

Miriam butted in, jumping from foot to foot. "After, you know—what happened to Jasmila, I knew I had to get out of that room, but the door was locked tight, as it always was. I managed to smash it open with the chair that was in the room—pretty solid, gold-plated, it came in handy. She looked like she was out for the count, but still, I was terrified the noise would wake her up. Then I was terrified someone would notice the state of the door and investigate, so I just tried to get away from there as fast as I could. I wanted to try and find you, but I didn't know where to go, I was turning into corridors left and right." She stopped for a moment to catch her breath and collect herself. I could see she was still red in the face. "Then, around one corner—SMACK!" She clapped her hands together. "I collided head-on with Narby here. Almost broke your nose as well as the pretty princess's, didn't I?"

He laughed politely and shook his head. "I was taken aback, but no damage done."

"I panicked, I just turned and ran—my first thought was

he knew what had happened to Jasmila and was looking for who was responsible."

"It was nothing like that," he said, picking up the threads of the tale in a measured counterpoint to Miriam's frantic delivery. "I was merely taking my afternoon stroll, as I have done every day. I'm staying in the palace while this unpleasantness is dealt with." I wasn't sure if he was referring to the war or to his betrothal to Jasmila. Probably both. "It's a fine old pile and I find there's so much to see, I come across something different every time. I often get lost myself, truth be told. Well, I called after Miriam here and asked what her hurry was, assured her she had nothing to fear from me. I knew you had suffered greatly in that last attempt to make Jasmila play along," he nodded at me, "but I didn't know that both of you were essentially being kept prisoner. It was an outrage to me, so I was only too happy to play my part in your reunion."

I nodded and grinned. I liked the prince a lot already. I was just glad someone was on our side, and thankfully he was the polar opposite of Jasmila.

"How did you know where I was being kept, then?" I asked.

"Luckily a passing guard happened to know, although it was still quite a struggle following his directions." He quirked an eyebrow. "Being royal has its uses, although I won't have all my princely privileges in this region until I marry Jasmila."

Wait, back up . . . we needed to deal with the most pressing issue here. "Someone's going to find her pretty soon, aren't they? The door's all bashed in. Or she wakes up. Either way, it's big trouble. We need to get our story straight."

The prince scratched his chin. "Well, Miriam could

claim that an anarchist forced their way into the room, attacked Jasmila and freed the prisoner. Then they fled again."

"No, no, that's not going to fly," I said, pacing around the bed. "First of all, where are the bits of the door when it got broken?"

"Well . . . they're outside in the hall," said Miriam. Her face fell as she put it together. "Oh . . ."

"Yeah, so if someone was smashing their way in from the outside, instead of the other way round, the pieces would be inside the room," I said. "And there's no other evidence of an attacker, how would they get past all the security?"

"I think the guards here leave something to be desired," mused Narby. "Back in my palace in Narbrutsi . . ."

"No, no, that's not it," I said, waving for him to be quiet with one hand. Thankfully he was mild-mannered enough to accept the interruption. I couldn't have done that with Jasmila, that was for sure. "I'm not worried about the guards, it's the princess. She knows where I'm being held. When she comes around, she's going to come straight for us!"

"We need to get out of here," said Miriam, glancing at the door as if expecting Jasmila to burst in then and there like some bloodied and battle-scarred warrior out for revenge.

"Right out of the palace, ideally, until we can figure out our next move." A thought hit me. "I was following her right up until the time you put her out of action." Miriam grinned. "If I stay alert, I should be able to know when she's coming around, at least while we're still in the same building."

Miriam nodded. "Any indication yet?"

"Nothing. Let's get moving." I started looking around to grab my belongings, before remembering I didn't have anything with me here, so it wouldn't take long for us to ship out. However, I then froze as I registered a blip that quickly escalated into a tsunami of rage and retribution. Fear grabbed me in a paralyzing grip, but I knew I had to use it to give me adrenaline and purpose.

"It's the princess! She's woken up. We have to go, now."

CHAPTER 12

We all barrelled out of the open door. "Let's take the stairs down to the ground floor," said Narby. "I know a side exit where I can get you out. There's a small hotel not far from the palace where you can hide out for now, I'll send you money for it."

There was a fair distance between my room and Miriam's. I wasn't sure we'd make it out of the palace before Jasmila discovered we'd fled, but I was hoping we could stay far enough ahead to give her the slip.

"Hey, what if she can follow us like you followed her?" asked Miriam as we hurried down flights of grand ornamental stairs. We passed a couple of guards on occasions who gave us quizzical looks, but the imperious presence of the prince seemed to be a get-out-of-jail-free card that let us pass unquestioned.

"I've got my guard up, so hopefully she won't break through," I panted. "I'm not following her every move like I was when she was in your room. It takes a lot of effort to do that without being detected, and it makes me more open to being breached. I know she's after us, and that's all I need to know right now."

A few seconds passed while we continued to move quickly down the floors. Then Miriam addressed the prince: "You know a lot about the palace and the city. Why? It's not your kingdom."

"It's going to be, though," he said. "Or it would be if this marriage ever goes ahead. This would become my residence, so like I said, I've been taking walks every day to familiarize myself with it. Also, it's nice to know if I'll ever need an escape route!"

"I can see how you might need one, being married to her," said Miriam with a grin in her voice. "I mean, that really is a selfless act. I can't imagine what it would be like."

"I was hoping she would warm to me in time," said the prince, perhaps misguidedly. "But even if not, this is for the good of the people. As a member of royalty, your role is to serve them. And I care about the people of this kingdom as much as I do my own."

"A shame their own princess doesn't seem to," I muttered.

"Very true. But I hope to bring some good governance and stability to this nation."

We were now on the ground floor, passing along a grander, higher corridor that possessed large doors leading to what were presumably grand halls, banqueting rooms, and ballrooms. One of them was where the intervention had taken place, but I wasn't sure which at this point. The prince nodded and smiled regally at more guards coming the other way.

Soon, we passed through a door that was smaller than the others and found ourselves in another corridor that was nowhere near as grand as the one we'd just left. The walls were covered in plaster that was chipped and flaking in places, and there were plain wooden doors, some of which had brass nameplates that had dulled and corroded. They looked like offices. We were probably in the administrative end of the operation, where all the work was done that actually kept the place going.

We went through a plain door at the end of the passage, and that was it, we were outside the palace. I blinked in the harsh winter sunlight. We'd only been in there for a few days, but with everything that had gone on it felt like we'd been imprisoned for months. Not quite safe yet, though— we were in the ornamental parade ground that enveloped the building with about a one-thousand-metre radius, which we had to cross to get to the railings at the other side. There was a small gate on this side, nowhere near as grand or imposing as the one at the front. A solitary guard stood sentinel, ramrod straight, making no indication that he'd seen us, although I didn't know how he could have failed to.

"Everyone's eyes adjusted?" I asked, squinting at my companions. "Come on, we'd better keep moving. The princess isn't close behind us, but it won't take her long."

We hustled quickly across the open ground while the soldier continued to give no response. I could see a few passers-by moving along the sidewalk beyond the railings and felt oddly exposed. I knew it was a thousand-to-one chance that someone would launch an attack similar to the one that had made the hole in the wall I'd seen when I first arrived, but I could feel my nerve endings tingling. In a short space of time, the palace had become a protective cocoon, but we weren't safe there any longer, not after what we'd done to the princess. We had to get away.

When we reached the guard, he bowed stiffly to the

prince, who said, "Afternoon, my good man. Would you be so kind as to open the gate for us?"

The man produced an ornate-looking key from the breast pocket of his uniform and turned to unlock the gate. This was proper old-school, ceremony stuff. Amazing really, the prince didn't yet have any real authority in this country, and yet people complied with anything he requested. He had an aura that naturally commanded respect.

A device beeped on the guard's waistband—a small oblong block with a small screen. As soon as he'd read the message, his fingers flew over the display as he sent one of his own, then he stopped unlocking the gate and turned around with a sick smile on his face. Other guards appeared, spewing out of the palace and running from the other gates, and we were quickly surrounded.

It was obvious what had happened—the princess had sent out orders preventing our escape. My arms were wrenched painfully behind my back, and I felt restraining devices click into place. Miriam and even Narby received the same treatment, and we were frogmarched back to the palace.

My thoughts detached themselves from what was happening as I considered what had led to this. It would be useless trying to escape from this latest situation. If only I'd bided my time while I was being held in that room, but I just hadn't liked being subject to the whims of a deranged sociopath—and look where it had gotten me. I doubted a comfortable room with a sumptuous bed waited for me now. And how would hiding out in a hotel room have got us any closer to achieving our goal of peace for this kingdom?

Because we would have been together. We could have plotted our next move. With Narby on our side, perhaps he could have interceded in a diplomatic way. The queen,

Jasmila's mother, wanted this marriage. They could have cooked up some ultimatum, threatened that Jasmila would be made destitute, her estates gone, if she didn't comply. That would get to her more than anything I could do. She'd been indulged and pampered too long—her entire life. A dose of reality was needed.

But there'd be no chance to plan now. We were taken back through the door we'd left from, and after passing along the same dingy corridors, we were shoved into a stairwell where we were huckled down a set of metal steps, the guards' boots clanging as we descended. This was it. No more luxury—we were being thrown into the dungeons, I guessed.

We exited the stairwell through a steel door. Harsh fluorescent lighting flickered overhead. We were marched along yet more passageways, these ones with a distinctly industrial air—stark grey walls and ceilings. At a junction up ahead, we were parted without a word—Miriam and Narby being taken to the right while I was steered left. I presumed they'd be split up too. We went past doors on each side with tiny iron grilles. Must have been cells—it was hard to tell, but they seemed empty, and I couldn't hear any sound. Where were the murderers, those who'd committed atrocities throughout this whole debacle? Was that allowed to continue unabated?

A few metres down one corridor, I was stopped outside one of the doors. One of the four guards surrounding me stabbed in a keycode on a panel next to the door, and it flew back soundlessly. They were considerate enough to remove my restraints before shoving me inside, where I stumbled but managed to keep my footing. No way was I going to show them any sign of weakness. The door swooshed back into place, and I heard nothing further—not even the grating sound of their footsteps that had been ringing in my ears just a few seconds before. It made sense these cells would be soundproofed if the padded ones we'd been held in upstairs were.

So, this was it, I'd hit rock bottom. Hard to see how I was going to get out of this one. I appraised my surroundings, which took just a few seconds. An iron bedframe with a thin, discoloured mattress. A plastic bucket in the corner. White walls greyed by years of neglect and another naked fluorescent light overhead—no windows, of course, it seemed like we were pretty far down in the bowels of the palace at this point.

I paced, scuffling my feet on the concrete floor—five steps one way, five steps the other, but it didn't help me come up with any plan. It seemed like I had pretty much zero chance now of finishing what I'd came here to do, and my stomach churned and twisted as a pervading sense of hopelessness sank its claws into me. The killing would continue, and I felt like it was on me. I also felt for Miriam because I didn't know what her fate would be. I loved her for what she'd done to Jasmila, but I hated myself for the consequences. A creature as vain as the princess, whose looks were her currency, wasn't going to just let it go after having her face bashed in, and I wasn't going to put anything past her.

And, of course, my mind was on my parents. They'd be beside themselves by now, and they must be here somewhere looking for us. But they knew what I'd been asked to do, so surely they'd come straight to the palace? What had happened to them?

So many unknowns. So much that my powers couldn't tell me. I needed guidance. Maybe I could speak to Mauritz and Kinfala again.

I gingerly stretched myself out on the mattress, adjusting slightly in an effort to stop various bumps and lumps from digging into me. I shut my eyes and tried to let go of everything around me and all other thoughts apart from of the place of peace where I had met them. I didn't know if I could do it. Last time, I'd been in a coma.

Sleep eluded me, however. Instead, I paced the cell until I was exhausted, trying to blot out all thoughts so I could fall into a deep sleep. A few hours later—I guessed so, anyway, not knowing the time—the slot on the door slid back, and a pair of gloved hands appeared holding a small tray with a plate of food and a water bottle. "Dinner," grunted a gruff male voice.

I took the tray, which contained some kind of stew, that gave off a pungent smell of greasy meat, and set it down on the mattress. "Do you know what's going to happen to me?" I asked the guard.

But the hands had retracted and there was no answer. I guessed he'd already walked off. I took a bite gingerly, but the meat was tough and gristly, and I could not identify the animal. I felt myself gag and spat the morsel out into the bucket. I took a welcome swig from the water bottle. At least they couldn't go wrong with that.

I set the tray in the corner of the cell and resumed my pacing. I wasn't hungry anyway. Rather, I was resentful. I'd been distracted from my task.

I walked until my eyelids grew heavy and time and space lost all meaning. I no longer saw the cell, but only the white expanse where I'd met Mauritz. That was good, I thought. It meant I was nearly there. I registered the bed out of the corner of my eye and collapsed onto it, no longer caring about the bumps. The next thing I knew, I *was* there —I knew it was real because of the all-pervading sense of tranquillity I recognized from last time. I let it repair my frazzled nerve endings and soothe my soul until I felt completely like myself again, like I could do anything. Only here did I get the sensation of being totally at ease. It was neither too cold, nor too warm. It was perfect.

But where were my friends? There was no one in sight. Could I will them to appear, or did I have to wait?

Then they were both in front of me. Did they know I'd be here? I hadn't met anyone else in this place yet, and it was perhaps an odd coincidence.

"Ah, Harica. It's so nice to see you again," said Kinfala, beaming a toothy smile that softened her eyes.

"Did you know I'd be here?" I asked, offering an awkward smile of my own, eyes flitting between her and Mauritz.

"My dear, we know when one of our own is in need of assistance," he said in that deep, warm voice, like a reviving cup of coffee on a freezing morning. "You're in dire straits, I know that much. Please, won't you tell us what troubles you, and we'll do everything we can to help."

I sighed. "Things aren't going to plan. Actually, they're going from bad to worse." I explained how I'd plotted for us to escape from Jasmila's clutches only to be caught and locked up again in much worse conditions. "If they try for another intervention, I can't see how it's going to be any different. She's going to make it even harder for me, and now she's got a grudge."

"Hmm . . ." said Kinfala, stroking her chin. "Is it really what you want to do, anyway? One day, this woman will be ruling the land as queen, and then everyone will see how ruthless she can be. I think she's managed to keep it quite well hidden up to now, but she can't sustain that forever."

I shrugged. "It's a political thing. The marriage is just

what has to happen for there to be peace between the two countries. It does seem backwards, like something out of the medieval history books. But I think, you know, once people have got this idea in their minds that something has to happen . . . they have to see it through. It's caught their imagination."

"But we know, at least," said Mauritz, indicating our small circle, "the marriage would be a sham. The prince does not love her—who could love such a creature? And it seems she's incapable of loving anything, apart from herself."

"I've met the prince," I said, thinking of the kindly, plain-speaking man who seemed willing to do anything for anyone. "He's very decent. And I think he's willing to, you know . . . sacrifice himself, sort of, for the sake of the greater good. He would make it work."

"I hear you, but let's bear in mind what Jasmila might be capable of. It's like throwing a mouse into the lion's den. She would conspire to end the marriage because it's not a situation she's chosen. Maybe she'd want to continue to appear respectable, but implicate the prince in something, make him look like the evil one . . . and then the fighting would start again, even worse than before."

"She's already doing that, remember. She says she has something on him but won't say what it is. It's totally shameless."

"Well, that's just the beginning. She'll make up worse accusations."

I considered. Mauritz had a lot invested in making sure this ended well. After all, he'd lost his life to this violence, this . . . mayhem between the two countries. An innocent victim caught in the crossfire. I had to get this right for his sake at least, so his death wouldn't be in vain . . . along with those of countless others. I felt responsibility settle on my shoulders like an iron bar, and the peace I'd felt upon returning to this place started to dissipate. I began to see there was only one way to truly resolve this.

"We need to expose Jasmila," I said slowly. "Let the people see who she really is . . . and then, she needs to go away. She's not fit to be ruler."

The two of them said nothing, watching me with their kind eyes and air of patience, giving me the time and space to formulate my thoughts. What would "going away" mean? Exile? But how could I arrange for such a thing? I was stuck in a prison cell, for one thing.

The only thing . . . no, it was probably nothing, but it might help to talk about it at least. Explore what it might mean. "You know how I was saying I was able to . . . hitch a ride with Jasmila, if you like, see what she was seeing. The first time, I didn't even realize it until afterwards. I thought it was a dream. I wonder if I could . . . do something more with it, you know, maybe influence her actions a bit? I was able to feel her emotions very powerfully, and I was able to mix my own anger with hers, rile her up even more."

I didn't know, though, it sounded outlandish even as I said it. Emotions were a blunt instrument. Something very visceral that didn't even need the use of words. Changing her thinking? That was a whole different ball game. I didn't know if I had that level of skill, or even if it was possible at all. That was if I could even reach her from where I was being kept. I'd tried already.

"My dear, you are capable of anything you put your mind to," said Kinfala, as if reading my mind—and she probably was, my confusion was likely flashing out like a firework display. "It just takes patience and application."

"Hmm, I don't know. I just want to get something done, get in and out, and normally I can do it."

"That's because you're young. This is going to take something more. It's not playground squabbles anymore. You've been called upon to do something great, Harica, and yes, it will need a lot from you, and it will probably take a lot out of you."

Boply. Well, I had to grow up sometime, might as well be now—but this sure was a massively complex and demanding way to do it.

But then, what was at stake if I didn't? More years of untold misery. I *had* to finish what I'd come here to do, in any way I could, regardless of whether I was stuck in a prison cell. How many more people would lose their lives or beloved family members if I didn't?

"It's hard to know where to start, though," I said. "I can't get a read on Jasmila from where I am at all. It's like by sending me down to that cell, she cut me off from the world physically but also on that . . . metaphysical plane, or whatever you want to call it."

The woman smiled, adding further crinkles to the creases that already lived at the corners of her eyes. "But that's not totally true, is it? Look around you." She gestured broadly. "This place is still available to you."

"Yeah . . . but I don't know if that can help me. Of course, you two have been a huge help, I didn't mean that," I added quickly, although they looked anything but offended. "I mean, could this place help me get to Jasmila? I don't even know if she knows this place exists. And if she did, would she want to visit? She doesn't seem like the sociable type, unless it's to get something she wants. And she doesn't use her powers for good, so I don't think she'd be interested in mixing with those who do."

"None of that matters. Her trace will be here. Her stamp, if you like, regardless of whether she knows about this place or not."

"How does that work?" I looked between the two of them, but Mauritz looked as curious as I felt. Of course, he was a relative newcomer here too.

"Well," she said, "this place is just a huge receptacle for the minds of those who can see beyond the everyday physical world. There's nothing real about it in a physical sense. Our bodies don't exist here and, of course, many of us have died in the corporeal plane, which is when we take up permanent residence." Mauritz nodded slowly. "We don't see each other's bodies but an approximation of them . . . the best versions of ourselves, if you like, how we want ourselves to be seen by the world."

Hmm, I liked the sound of that. A good way of dealing with any unwanted lumps or blemishes if nothing else.

"So, we're all connected here, even when we're *not* here, in a purely visual sense I mean. You yourself didn't know about this place until you left your home and travelled to the planet. We were here when you needed us."

"But in a way," added Mauritz, "you were always here. So was I, even though I hadn't considered using my power for half a century. I thought it was a curse to shut off and forget about. But here, I've learnt how beautiful it can be, and that I should have made more use of it—for good."

I remained silent for the time being, drinking in everything they were saying. I too often thought of my power as a curse—especially recently when it had landed me in so much trouble. But I'd never been through anything like what Mauritz had experienced, and maybe I'd do well to remember that. I still had a chance to do incredible things with my gift.

"You certainly do," said Kinfala, and I blushed at being so naked with my thoughts and feelings. There was no hiding anything from these two. But maybe that was a good thing too. Back home, I was so used to throwing up this big front, acting like my gift was no big deal when it was such a big drain on my own mental energy. Hopefully that wouldn't happen if I could learn to wield it better. And it definitely was a good thing to be more open, especially with those who understood.

"Okay, so let's get down to it," I said, suddenly feeling fired up. "Jasmila is here somewhere? Or I can use this place to get to her, somehow? How do I start?"

"Well, I don't know her, so it would be much harder for me to find her," said Kinfala. "But you have a big advantage. You've met her in the real world, even been inside her mind, so you just have to tune into her . . . signature, if you like. You'll know it when you find it."

"Hmm. I read somewhere that everyone has their own unique scent. Is it a bit like that?"

"Yes! Or a fingerprint. There's no disguising or faking that."

"I get it." I closed my eyes and tried to summon up what it had been like to be inside Jasmila's mind. It definitely seemed like it had a strong signature—I'd felt arrogance, self-confidence, an almost callous disregard for others—but while it had been overwhelming at the time, trying to recreate it after the fact was a struggle. It felt like trying to get a handhold on the side of a mountain that was smeared in honey.

CHAPTER 13

"You know, I think it's better if this is something you do on your own," I heard Kinfala say, and I opened my eyes. "To find the mind of another, you need to go deep into your own." They both smiled, and then faded almost instantly in front of me.

Her words were left ringing in my ears—I had to go deep into my mind if I wanted to find Jasmila's. Hmm, introspection wasn't exactly my favourite pastime, if that's what was called for. Going into other people's minds took a lot out of me, so I'd never felt the need to explore my own.

At least it was easy to tune out the external noise, with the absence of any sights or sounds in the blank space around me. I decided to try lying down, which seemed a bit disconcerting with the lack of any discernible floor, but I was standing up okay—and once I did it, I found I was just as comfortable as in my bed at home.

Taking a deep breath in through my mouth, and blowing it out through my nose, I started again. I soon found it wasn't the external noise that was the problem, it was everything going on inside—thoughts of Miriam, our parents, Narby, what had happened to me in the space shuttle, all the killing that had gone on in the name of this crazy princess. In fact, this was going to be much harder than I could have suspected because once the outside world was removed, all that stuff was given free play to jump around the inside of my head, like a bunch of frogs in a badly sealed box that were getting agitated and trying to burst the lid off.

I was doing this for them. That's what I had to remember. If I didn't do something to alter Jasmila's course, all this insanity would just continue.

So, I visualized myself going past all the faces I knew, smiling at them and allowing them to give me a nod of encouragement, then moving on. The hope was that if I gave a bit of airtime to each one, I could then put them away, compartmentalize them, and concentrate on the search for Jasmila. Like I was setting off on a journey and they were wishing me well.

Once I'd done that, I felt a bit more of a sense of purpose. It was like I was completely still, and I summoned up all the energy I could muster and threw it into trying to recreate what it had been like to be inside Jasmila's mind.

All that avarice, that malice, the self-driven callous disregard for others . . . if the mental landscape was like a scent, then hers was a particularly strong one, which was a big help at least.

There it was! I tracked onto her signature and was suddenly inside her mind looking out. Just like I had been before... but this time, I had to go further because I had to try to control her actions. I felt like I could do it—I'd become so still and silent in trying to reach her that I'd managed to creep up like an unobserved assassin. I felt invisible, and there was a power in that. The important thing was not to show my hand now.

So where were we? In Jasmila's room again, apparently. Her boudoir, I suppose you could call it, all silk sheets and effortless luxury. The princess was lying on those sheets, super relaxed, playing some game on a handheld device. I detected a dull ache around her nose area and smiled inwardly as I remembered how Miriam had done a number on her. That pretty little schnozz must have been broken.

I was glad I'd found her in a seeming state of downtime because it meant there was nothing else around to distract her. It must be the evening, although I'd totally lost track of time by now. But what should be my next move? Would there be any incriminating evidence in this room, and if so, how was I going to find it? Even if I could do it—and I wasn't sure I could—I didn't think I should make her get up and suddenly start rifling through drawers. If I was going to pull this off, anything I made her do had to seem like a natural thing to her.

And I didn't have infinite time. My body had to eat. I hadn't gone into a coma again, and I'd get woken up when they delivered food to my cell.

Then it hit me—of course, I didn't need to find physical evidence. I wasn't an investigator trying to fit her up the old-fashioned way, I was right inside her mind, I had access to her memory and thought processes if I knew how to look. Then, depending on what I found, hopefully I could influence her actions. I just had to be careful about it.

Mentally I was holding my breath. I felt like I was listening behind a door and trying to remain as still as possible so I wouldn't be detected.

I looked at the game on the device she held in her hand. It was a pretty simple arrange-the-blocks puzzle kind of thing, the sort of game I hadn't played since I was seven or eight. The princess might like to give off an air of sleek sophistication, but it seemed like her pastimes were pretty juvenile. She was winding down, and she would probably be asleep soon. Maybe I should wait. It would be easier to rummage around if she wasn't conscious at the time.

After a while, Jasmila yawned, laid the device down on the elegantly carved side table, and rose from the bed. She padded to the ensuite bathroom and flipped on the light. I tried to tune out of the next part as much as I could—she was entitled to her privacy, after all—but if I was going to have any hope of achieving something here, I had to stick with it. While she was washing her hands and peering at herself in the mirror, grimacing at the state she was in—her nose was encased in a bandage held in place by another one tied around her head, and a gauze pad covered the hit she'd taken to the temple—I tried to discern if there was any sign of other life behind her eyes, and couldn't see any. I was doing a good job of staying hidden so far.

She returned to the main room, changed into one of those frilly, revealing silk nightgowns I'd seen her in before, got into bed and flipped off the bedside light. I bided my time, waiting for her body to slow down to the simplest functions, breathing and temperature regulation. I kept still and unobserved, waiting for her to go into proper REM sleep and for her brain to start sorting through her day and translating it into dreams. That large-scale production playing out would hopefully give me enough cover to start looking through things properly.

Once I was sure she was in as deep a slumber as possible, I started to feel my way around. There was the part of the brain that controlled her senses, the part that controlled movement, the part that regulated temperature . .

. I didn't know all the technical terms, but words like "cerebellum" and "cortex" suggested themselves to me. The part that contained the blueprint for her personality was at the front. I was going with "frontal lobe." Lashings of arrogance, superiority, a sense that others were beneath her or perhaps didn't really count as proper people. Our princess seemed to have a lot of the traits you'd associate with a psychopath or at least a sociopath.

But was there anything I could use against her? I got deeper in and eventually found her memory stores, but one thing that quickly became clear was that it wasn't simply a case of looking through a well-ordered filing cabinet. It was a mess, with vague sensations, scenes, and bits of dialogue floating past, such as Jasmila berating her butler for not serving her Clunchian oysters at the desired temperature. Obviously, what was most prominent was today's events, as the brain was processing whatever had happened to her that day, and I grew still and tried to tune in. I could sense the princess's fury that we'd managed to escape, and the fact it was with the help of her would-be future husband only rubbed salt into the wound. Nice gesture on his part, but it would no doubt only be harder to persuade her to marry him now. Then there was the glee that came with our recapture, and the sense that a right had been wronged, that equilibrium had been restored, at least as far as the princess was concerned.

These recent memories were very visceral and almost cloying in their vividness. I tried to duck under them to get at something deeper. Again, I had to concentrate hard and, even though it was basically a muscle memory, I felt like I was holding my breath. I saw Jasmila at five years old, trying on a pair of lavishly expensive pink shoes encrusted with diamonds. Obviously, that was a major milestone. Then something stopped me in my tracks. I saw Jasmila as a teenager, being sexually assaulted by one of the guards, and I couldn't help instantly flashing back to what happened in the space shuttle. For the first time, I felt a pang of empathy for her, as it seemed like we had something else in common that I hadn't expected. It didn't look like Jasmila used her gift to stop the attack. Had she even known about it at that point? So many questions. Maybe this incident could help explain her hardened attitude to the world.

Then I gasped as I remembered how she'd read my mind when I was lying with a drip in my arm in that comfortable room, when I'd thought about exposing what happened to me in the space shuttle. She hadn't even batted an eyelid, despite the same thing—worse, actually—happening to her. Wow, she really was cold. Not a hint of female empathy or solidarity. Everything was purely about furthering her own agenda.

Regardless of that, clearly this assault wasn't something I could use against her. There had to be something more here beyond the obvious. Did everything that ever happen to us get stored? Perhaps, although a lot of it was probably irretrievable, unless something happened that dredged it up, or else it related to the hundreds or probably thousands of basically indistinguishable days where nothing of note happened.

So probably it was better to look at things that were significant. That's where the juicy stuff would be found. I stayed still and tried to tune in again and found that what was significant to Jasmila mostly seemed to involve money. Buying wardrobes full of designer dresses. Investing in stocks and shares and megabucks tech companies. Ludicrously expensive bottles of Tyrolean champagne. Not that surprising really—she was a shallow and superficial creature. But maybe there was something to do with where the money came from that I could use. It was the royal family, so it was funded by the taxpayer more or less. But was all of that above board? Had the princess been helping herself to more than her fair share?

I didn't know and, even if she was, it probably didn't seem wrong to her due to her twisted perception of things, so there was nothing that stood out. Trying to examine someone's memory wasn't like looking through a bank statement, with everything accounted for neatly. It was totally vague and abstract. But it felt like that's where I should focus my attention: money, something that was obviously important to her. It was a starting point, anyway.

I felt like I'd been here long enough, and she'd probably start to awaken soon. I picked my way backwards carefully, wanting my retreat to be as unobtrusive as my entrance had been. Tomorrow, I'd return when she was awake and take on a much more difficult task: trying to control her actions so I could find something that would incriminate her. She might wonder why she was doing it, of course, but hopefully that wouldn't matter if it was enough to bring her under investigation. I wanted *her* to feel what it was like to be locked up at someone else's whim.

But for now, I had to come back to myself, back to that cell, so I was awake when they brought me breakfast, whatever that would consist of. It couldn't appear like I was up to anything. Leaving the princess to her sleep, I came back to my own mind, where I enjoyed a few hours' sleep of my own, even if it was a bit fitful, waking and then dropping off again.

CHAPTER 14

I woke and stayed awake about an hour before breakfast—I guessed. I still had no means of telling the time or even whether it was night or day in this subterranean dungeon. I thought over whether I was doing the right thing, whether the princess might suspect anything, whether I was pushing things too far. I still needed to go a lot further with her than I had until now, and every ounce of my skill would be called upon. I paced in my cell: such a cliché for a prisoner, but it sure helps you think. I'd come this far, and I had to carry on, or else all my efforts up to now would be for nothing. I stopped and stretched my arms, then decided to try some distinctly wobbly push-ups. My physique was less than drassic, but I thought maybe if I got some physical exercise, it would help strengthen my mental faculties for the task that lay ahead. I'd been working my brain out a lot, but I'd never been the biggest fan of exerting myself physically, and I'd noticed how out of puff I'd gotten when we were trying to escape from the palace. I was sure being in a coma hadn't helped.

I was trying to recover from a rather pitiful attempt at a

sit-up when the hatch on my door slid back and the gloved hands extended a small tray, on which sat a plastic bowl and cup, both chipped and worn. A rather depressing aroma of burnt porridge wafted into the room. I pulled myself to my feet, staggered over to the door and took the tray from the outstretched hand, which then retreated. "Thanks, dude," I said in what was meant to be a cheerful, sing-song voice, but it came out strangled and choked the way it does when you haven't spoken out loud for a while. Of course, there was no reply.

I drank the water down in one gulp because I had become quite dehydrated and my throat was parched, but I only picked at the porridge, which it seemed had been deliberately prepared badly. After my exercise, I was hungry, but it seemed like my plan to keep myself in peak condition wasn't matched by my jailers. I pushed the bowl to the side and lay back on the mattress.

Closing my eyes, I homed in on Jasmila's signal again, with which I was now familiar. It was like slipping into a second skin, although I didn't want to get too comfortable inside her mind. She was still asleep, which I probably should have expected—although I didn't know the time, it was no doubt still early, and the princess likely wasn't someone who worked to anyone else's schedule.

I waited patiently, trying to figure out how I could influence her actions, poking around the hypothalamus, although I wouldn't know if anything was working until she was conscious. It seemed to take a while, but eventually her eyes opened and she yawned and stretched in what I could only describe as an extremely elegant and ladylike way. Interesting—it was like she was putting on a front from the moment she woke up, donning a veneer of sophistication to hide the ugliness underneath. I knew all too well what she was really like.

I let her go through her morning routine—you know, the stuff we all do before we actually present ourselves to the world—trying my utmost to do the mental equivalent of looking the other way and whistling through the most intimate parts of it. I could admit the princess was a beautiful woman with a stunning figure, even despite the battered face, but spying on her in that kind of way definitely wasn't my game. It was the corruption, what was going on beneath the surface that I was looking to expose.

I did listen to her thoughts, though. It seemed like she was planning to meet with a couple of other women for lunch. Hard to pick up on exactly who they were, but I didn't think the princess had real friends exactly—maybe stylists, accountants, general attendants, and hangers-on. Obviously, it would be within the palace because she wasn't venturing out at the moment, what with the volatile, explosive nature of the streets outside—something I was in no doubt she was directly responsible for, and I was willing to bet it went deeper than this sham marriage I was supposed to be facilitating.

Once she was (thankfully) dressed in a sharply tailored pantsuit—baby pink, of course, matching an air of driven sophistication with the childlike innocence she loved to convey—and was idly buffing her nails, I mused about whether I could try to stop her going, but then decided against it. There was a chance I could pick up something to use against her, some juicy tidbit she let slip while chatting candidly with people she thought were her confidants. It was a punt, of course, because it was just as likely—or more so—that she'd be keeping whatever she was up to to herself, but there was no harm seeing what the appointment might bring. And there were a few hours till then, so it gave me a chance to poke around her inner sanctum to see what I could turn up. Or rather, to get her to do that without arousing suspicion about why she was doing it—how easy would it be?

Also, the lunch thing might not come off because I didn't know when my own next miserable offering was going to be shoved through the door. I had to be there to take it so I didn't arouse any suspicion. No, I had to see what I could do now.

As unobtrusively as I could, I let my own thoughts come into play and merge with hers gradually, and as seamlessly as possible. It wasn't like the encounter with Miriam when Jasmila was in a heightened state and I could use that as a shield to operate behind. She was relaxed and in her own space, and it was absolutely crucial not to arouse any suspicion that anything was amiss.

I tried to transmit a feeling of doubt, that she'd lost something and had to try to find it while not being totally sure what it was. You know, that kind of nagging sensation when you think you're meant to be doing something but can't put your finger on what. That was all I had because obviously I didn't know what I was looking for, but ideally I would find something incriminating that would be a starting point for taking the princess down. Knocking her off her perch.

Because she was sitting in her favourite place, in front of the mirror, I had the pleasure of seeing a brief frown cross her battle-worn features as she put down the nail file and started rifling the drawers on each side of the dresser, while not being totally aware of why she was doing so. *Go on, break a nail, that would be even better.*

At first all she found—or all I found, rather—were

various items of saucy underwear that didn't bear too close of an inspection. I tried to gloss over those as quickly as I could. Then the next drawer down was cluttered with lip glosses, makeup compacts, false eyelashes and various other items of beauty paraphernalia, all crammed in any old way. Certainly nothing of interest to me. It seemed the princess was pretty messy under the polished exterior she liked to present. Obviously, I needed something a bit more incriminating than that, but I was still enjoying the confusion I glimpsed on her face as she rummaged through her own drawers for no obvious good reason.

Then in the last drawer on the right-hand side, I found something a bit more interesting—a dusty old book, plain black cover with a creased and worn spine. Some sort of notebook or diary? It seemed curiously old-fashioned at a time when most were happy putting their innermost thoughts out there for the universe to see on the various interplanetary social platforms. The princess was an extrovert, and I knew she did the same—I'd checked her accounts. So, what would she be doing with an old book that looked like it should belong in some museum?

There was only one way to find out. I transmitted the message through her brain to get her fingers to open the book and start going through the pages. I couldn't make sense of what I was seeing at first—there were just columns of names and dates, with figures alongside them. Prompting her to turn the pages, we went through five, six, seven sheets of the same thing. None of the names immediately meant anything to me, but then I saw something that almost made me lose my grip on Jasmila's subconscious. I had to pull myself back or I would end up showing my hand.

Mauritz Spindelman.

I pictured the friendly relative whose existence I'd

known nothing of before his death but whom I'd come to love. What connection could he have to this loathsome creature, other than that they both shared the same gift I had? I didn't think Jasmila had accessed that astral plane, or whatever, where I'd met Mauritz and his friend. She didn't seem like the type who was interested in meeting those who shared her power. Certainly, if she'd met my friends, they hadn't told me—and I didn't know why they wouldn't share that information.

I thought about Mauritz. The only reason I knew of his existence was because he'd been murdered.

Jasmila's attention had wandered. I could tell she was irritated and suspicious. I couldn't linger for long. Getting her to refocus her attention on the book in her hands, I looked at the names that were near Mauritz's. None of them immediately meant anything to me, but then I saw one that seemed to call out, almost waving its hands to attract my attention. It was an unusual name, but I'd almost forgotten it when I'd noticed Mauritz's, for obvious reasons. Gardano Haslamtether.

And I knew, the same way I knew my heart was pumping blood round my body, that I'd seen both names the first time in close proximity on a page, the same way I was seeing them now. It was the report where I'd read that Mauritz had been killed. There'd been what, seven in total? That was awful I didn't know that for sure, just because I'd been intrigued by the sight of my own name. Each was an individual, no doubt with family members who cared about them and missed them deeply. And each had lost their life in a senseless act of violence. I thought I recognized a couple of names, but I couldn't be a hundred percent. Haslamtether was what stood out to me.

I slid Jasmila's eyes over to the figures that appeared

alongside the names. Monetary figures? The dollar sign wasn't there, but I couldn't see what else it could be. Mauritz's was 2500. Haslamtether's was 2800. Were these paltry figures supposed to be what each of these lives was worth? What the hell was going on here?

It could only mean one thing. Jasmila was implicated in the murders, but why and how? Was she receiving money for each one, or were these the amounts she was paying for each hit?

I didn't know, but I was going to find out. One thing was for sure, I wouldn't be a party to the union between the princess and Narbert. He was a nice guy and didn't deserve to be dragged into this madness . . . whatever it was. The princess was supposed to be part of a peaceful solution to the violence, but all the while she was stoking its flames and possibly profiteering from it.

In fact, my path now seemed clear. Jasmila could never be in a position where she could ascend to the throne of Camzhargi. She was a maniac who clearly wasn't fit to rule —if that was how callously she treated the lives of her own subjects, what else might she be capable of once she was in full command?

I didn't know how I was going to do it, but Jasmila needed to be exiled or imprisoned. That seemed like something that would be a tall order for an outsider who was imprisoned herself, but then I wasn't strictly stuck here, was I? I had some control over the princess, as long as I continued to play it careful and not give myself away. And I had access to the other plane where I could get advice from my friends.

Poor Mauritz. I had to get justice for him and find out what really happened. I knew all the victims deserved that, but Mauritz was a personal connection I could latch onto for motivation. He hadn't even made use of his gift for most of his life, believing it to be more of a curse than a blessing because of one unfortunate incident. I couldn't undo his death, but I could show him how much good such a gift could do by unseating the princess from her position of power. She clearly thought she was unassailable, and I was going to show her that her actions were going to come back to bite her in the posterior.

I tuned out of her mind and readjusted to the dingy surroundings of my cell, stretching out as comfortably as I could on the lumpy mattress to consider my next move. Let her go to lunch. Let her enjoy her fancy life and her privileges, be in a false state of security until it all got snatched away. I had to be careful not to do anything that seemed too jarring. She might be wondering why she got out that notebook to look through it, but then she probably got a kick out of it, gloating over the lives she'd stolen and apparently getting away with it. I pictured her putting back the book and finishing going about beautifying herself. More like putting lipstick on a pig. No doubt she was smug in the knowledge she was causing untold grief and misery but then would be hailed as this great saviour once she finally agreed to the marriage. And she was playing a game, seeing how long she could drag it out—otherwise my intervention wouldn't have been needed.

Well, her game was about to come crashing down around her ears.

CHAPTER 15

I lay back and let my mind explore the possibilities. I could influence Jasmila to release me from captivity, but I was probably safer here where I was less likely to be suspected. Of course, she knew about my gift, but she didn't realize how far it could go. By being out of the way, at least as far as she saw it, I could stay under the radar.

I had to work fast—no point hanging about. At any time she could spring us out of here and try to have us investigated, and then I wouldn't have all this wonderful free time I was having now.

A loud knock and a "hey" startled me. Must have dozed off with all the excitement. The gloved hands had extended themselves into the room again, holding another tray. I wondered what delights were in store for me this time. Getting up from the bed, I caught a whiff of burnt cabbage —and indeed, the plate seemed to contain some kind of indeterminate stew with a blackened, singed vibe to it. I took it and the cup of water and retreated to the bed. "Sorry about that. You woke me up," I called conversationally, but the tray was already being retracted through the door slot and I heard footsteps moving away.

The stew was like chewing on an old boot, but at least there was a decent amount. I hadn't realized how hungry I was after the thin gruel I'd been given earlier.

I decided to leave the princess alone until the evening. Part of me didn't want to miss anything, but my more pragmatic side told me not to risk showing my hand. I might dip in at different times during the day, get a feel for her routine if there was any. The only way I had of marking time was the meals they brought—there wasn't even a window down here for me to get a feel for the changing light. I lay back and tried to let sleep take me again until the evening meal arrived, but it didn't work. I just kept thinking of Miriam and our parents. In different ways, they'd be worried sick and wondering what was going to happen next. The guilt nibbled away at me like when you've got an itch that doesn't seem to go away no matter how much you scratch. I tried to tell myself it was for the people who were suffering and dying, but despite Mauritz, that felt weirdly abstract when I didn't know them at all. I didn't know if I was putting my friend and our families through all this without any sort of reward at the end.

My churning thoughts were interrupted again by the arrival of dinner. Probably a good thing.

I had no idea if the gloved hands belonged to the same person each time, but I took the tray off them and said, "Thanks again. By the way, we have got to stop meeting like this." An aroma of overboiled vegetables hit my nostrils as I regarded the offering—strips of an unidentified pinkish meat and a jumble of soggy carrots and broccoli. I sat down and started eating. I'd really have rather cast it aside, but the meals were filling a hole, and I needed all my energy because I was planning on paying the princess another visit after dinner.

When I'd finished, I sat the plate down next to the other crockery I'd accumulated. I was going to have to try to give them back because the smell was already getting obnoxious in the small room with no ventilation. No matter—for now I was going to the part of the palace where opulence and luxury existed, obnoxious in a different way.

I lay back down and closed my eyes, hunting for Jasmila's mental signature that was now familiar to me. It didn't take long as I found her in her lair again, hunched over her dresser. As she looked down, I saw I'd tuned in just in time. There was the book again—the one I'd found earlier —and the princess was writing in three new names, apparently based on the content of an infochip message.

Well. There'd been three new murders. And now I had incontrovertible proof that Jasmila had a hand in the mayhem. It wasn't like this was just a list she was looking after for someone, although that would be incriminating enough.

The names didn't mean anything to me, although of course they would mean something to someone and probably quite a few people. Yet the princess treated them as if they were merely pieces of data, so casually writing them in her little book alongside figures that, while substantial, couldn't reflect the worth of a human life.

She cast her eye briefly up the list of names that had already been filling up the page and returned the book to its place in the drawer. Keeping her palm open in front of her, she flicked away from the message thread—the author of the other half of the conversation was represented by a codeword, not a name, although I couldn't guess at its meaning.

Then she went to another thread, this one with Nathaniel, that clerk she was carrying on with. It looked like he'd messaged about half an hour before, asking to meet up. The message was blunt and to the point, not including any gooey declarations or saucy double entendres. Maybe that was the way she liked to keep the communication just in case anyone tried to hack the messages. The irony of that thought wasn't lost on me, but I was frustrated I couldn't flip back and read the earlier texts —not to satisfy my own need for gossip but to see if there was anything more incriminating I could use against the princess.

Clearly, she'd been in no rush to reply to him as she calmly administered to her murder tally, but now she sent back the brief message: "OK be at the room in 15 mins."

He replied: "I'll be there. I need to tell u smthing."

Jasmila paused a few seconds before replying: "OK but not in the mood for too much talk if u know what I mean xxx."

Clearly her last message was her trying to be sweet and seductive, so the communication wasn't always just functional. I was interested in what he had to say, but I'd be tuning straight out if any shenanigans started. I'm not a pervert.

She made her way through the passage and into the room where she'd so recently had a showdown with Miriam. The door had been repaired, the place had been scrubbed, and there were no signs of any kind of struggle. Nathaniel was standing behind the bed, arms crossed, and she was clearly surprised by his stance. So was I. What was going on?

She came round the bed, draping her hand along the sheets.

"Don't touch me!" he said as she reached out to touch his arm. He didn't jump back or anything like that, he stayed rooted in place. He looked completely immovable.

"What's wrong?" she said in a voice that sounded like it had been dipped in syrup. Although I obviously couldn't see her face, I could just tell she was doing her best puppy dog eyes.

"This has got to stop," he said, looking at her with his face screwed up. I could read disdain and disgust that he wasn't even trying to conceal.

I felt her demeanour harden, and she laughed harshly. "Well, my dear, you don't exactly get to decide that. Unless you want to find out what happens to those who reject me."

"I don't mean just *this*," he said, waving a hand at the room—a throwaway gesture that seemed to encapsulate the tawdry and sordid nature of their affair. "I mean, the war. The fighting. The killing. It's totally senseless. You need to marry that prince and bring an end to this madness. Actually be a leader to these people."

She scoffed and straightened her back, crossing her arms to mirror his stance and cover her cleavage. "So now you take the moral high ground? It never bothered you before as long as you were getting your piece of Jasmila. Well, let me tell you, you've had your last slice. I have no intention of marrying that insufferable prince, but I'll need to find another plaything to keep me occupied."

"My brother is dead!" he roared. He uncrossed his arms and shifted on the spot, looking like he was barely restraining himself from closing the gap between them and throttling her. "In the latest attack. He was out with his friends, celebrating one of their birthdays. I don't know how it happened; they don't even report that anymore. Just the names. That's all they are to you. But they're not just names, they're people, and they're being blown to bits. It would have been a bomb. He goes out for a celebration, and he ends up in pieces on the pavement. It's got to stop, and you're the one who can do that. You need to stop it now."

"Look, okay . . . I'm sorry about your brother," she said, reaching out a hand. I couldn't detect any remorse on her part, though. What I could feel was her synapses firing up, as she thought desperately of how she could placate him and keep things going the way she wanted them. She was heartless.

He flinched away from her, edging towards the door. "See, this . . . I can't justify this anymore. It was fun and all that, as long as I didn't think about what was going on outside these walls. But these are people with families—I've spoken to my mother and she's completely distraught. I want you to go and speak to that prince now, get this sorted out."

She looked down at the floor for a moment and then back up, pinning him with her eyes. "I know our relationship has been strictly physical, you could say, rather than based on deep and meaningful conversations . . . but I think one thing you've learned about me is that you do *not* get to tell me what to do. I'll think of another way to stop this."

"How?" he demanded, his eyes blazing. "The marriage is what the people want. It's symbolic, the two sides coming together. Maybe it won't totally stop all the killing, who knows, but it's something you can definitely do that will make a difference. It's time to step up."

"You don't tell me what to do," she repeated, but her wheels were spinning. She was sounding like a petulant toddler. To me, it didn't seem like there was anything she could do to improve the situation—except the one thing she was so absolutely dead set against.

"Look, this is how it's going to happen," he said, making a sweeping gesture with his hand. I was starting to believe he was the one who was coming out on top, although I still couldn't tell which way this would go. "If you don't agree to marry the prince, I'm going to go and find your mother and tell her what's been happening between us—maybe not every little detail," he sneered, "but I'll say you're going to make amends for it by going ahead with the marriage. If you don't do it after that, I'll need to go wider, go through the media, try to shame you into it. It'll still work if people can see you've seen the error of your ways."

She shook her head. "Actually, you won't be doing any of that." Before I could register what was going on, she took a quick step towards the table at the side of the bed and pulled out a horrendous-looking knife.

It all happened before I could properly register it. He wasn't near enough to the door and was taken by surprise, so he couldn't defend himself. She darted up close, pulled her hand back and stabbed him through the heart, not just once but three, four, five times, in a desperate frenzy, blood spattering the front of her nightdress. I wanted to look away, but there was nowhere else to go—it was like being stuck on the same streaming channel. More than the carnage, it was his eyes that gripped me, pinning me in place. Frozen wide with horror while his mouth worked soundlessly. He remained pinned against the wall while she kept stabbing like a woman possessed but slithered to the floor when she pulled the knife out for the last time, leaving a wet trail of blood.

Time slowed down as Jasmila contemplated the lifeless

body in front of her with what seemed like a horrifyingly clinical detachment. I wanted to tear my eyes away, but it was hers I was looking through. For the first time in a while, I became aware of my own body back in the cell, my stomach curdling as my thoughts drifted to what the implications might be for me. I'd remained hidden for now, but I'd almost forgotten myself a moment ago with the horror of what had just unfolded. If she discovered I'd been in her head and seen this . . . A chill ran down my back that was like a blast of cold wind. She was capable of anything, that was crystal clear to me now.

Another thought materialized in my mind, so clearly it seemed to have physical form.

This monstrosity should never be queen.

She still held the knife in her right hand. At that moment she looked down to see the blood beginning to congeal on the shaft. I wasn't sure whether she'd looked of her own will or how much I'd influenced it.

There was nothing to work with now. I'd thought it earlier, but now I knew I couldn't, in all conscience, meet with Jasmila and Narbert again and try to engineer an agreement. What would I be condoning? And the thought of being in her presence again physically was like an iron flower unfolding itself inside me slowly and paralyzing my vital parts. What if she knew that I knew and was waiting on the right moment to act on it, lulling me into a false sense of security?

The hand holding the knife began to rise slowly, although I wasn't sure why. I felt surprise on Jasmila's part too, and lack of control. Something else was clawing its way to the surface: self-loathing. I sensed it was normally kept well-hidden and now the curtain had fallen away. It was a vulnerable feeling, it seemed malleable, and I knew I'd found her Achilles' heel.

The knife was now in front of her throat and she was squinting down at it. Her eyes flicked once quickly to the body and then back to the knife, and then it shot towards her neck like a spring that had been pulled too far and then snapped back to its original shape.

More blood, spurting out like escaping steam. Jasmila's vision went blurry and she dropped to her knees. I was dizzy and disoriented, making it hard to grasp what was going on, but something was falling away. Almost like a sense of release amid the carnage. Jasmila's eyes closed once and she seemed to force them open again, then they fell shut a second time and everything stayed black. Next thing I knew, I was staring at the ceiling in my cell.

The connection was gone. And I knew why. Jasmila had killed herself . . . and I'd been there to witness the final moments.

CHAPTER 16

With traumatizing images flooding my brain, I hauled myself off the bed and paced around the room to try to clear my head. It felt compressed, like I'd been caught up in a tidal wave and thrown this way and that, unable to breathe. That wasn't the way I'd seen things playing out. I remember having that thought—so stark—that Jasmila couldn't be queen. But for that to come through her death? I hadn't engineered that, had I?

Was I a killer?

And poor Nathaniel. I definitely hadn't had anything to do with that, that was all her. My stomach had lurched when that happened. But after that . . . that was where it all went muddy. I remember Jasmila's surprise when she turned the knife on herself. Why would she be surprised at her own action? And then the self-loathing, like a living, writhing thing. A wounded animal trapped in a bag, fighting to get out. I'd untied that bag. Had I manipulated Jasmila's self-hatred to drive her to the ultimate end?

I couldn't be sure. And that terrified me.

If my gift had taken over and seized an advantage when

I saw it, that meant it had a mind of its own. It meant it was evil, and I'd taken a life, just as Jasmila had. Was I evil? I didn't want to go there, it was easy to say it was the gift, it wasn't me. But then it wasn't easy to say that. It was a part of me, inseparable for as long as I could remember.

If my gift made me a killer, I had to suppress it and keep it down for good. I could never risk it getting out of control again. I wished it could be cut out, physically removed like a cancer, but I knew that wasn't possible, so I was still going to have to live with it. It would just be in its box and kept under lock and key.

That lack of control I felt . . . I never wanted to feel like that again. I didn't want to feel like I had the power to influence someone to take their own life. What if it was more than just the gift? What if some darker part of my nature had taken over, simply used the gift as a tool to achieve what it wanted?

I shook my head. Thinking like that was going to get me tied up in knots. I couldn't believe that I really was evil or it would drive me insane.

Time to focus on the practicalities. What would happen next? With Jasmila gone, did that mean any chance of a reconciliation between the two sides was gone too? I hoped not. What I needed to do was make people see that the marriage would not have offered a solution. Jasmila would still have been scheming and manipulating, tearing people's lives apart for her own benefit.

I hadn't meant to kill her, but the country was better off without her. Everyone would see that soon. I didn't know who'd end up running the country, but Narbert had shown himself to be extremely decent. Maybe there was some way he could be brought in as future king. Obviously, I didn't know all the technicalities involved there.

How long would it be before I was let out of here? Jasmila had to be discovered first, and then all hell would break loose. I just hoped I didn't get forgotten about. And Miriam too. She was an innocent bystander in this, I'd put her through a ton of flam on this whole trip.

It was late at night now. The two doomed lovers would have to lie in repose until the morning, and then they'd be looking for Jasmila when it was seen she wasn't in her quarters. Had to guess no one knew about the passageway to the room next door, except the person who installed it, but Nathaniel got into the room the normal way. It wasn't like there was no other way in, and they'd be checking everywhere. Given the room was two doors along, it shouldn't take them too long.

I didn't remember falling asleep, my mind was totally wired on adrenaline and my thoughts were working overtime, but I must have burned out because the next thing I heard was a banging on the door and a voice yelling "Breakfast!" I lurched off the bed, but that was a bad move because the room was spinning around me in a blurry haze and I wobbled on my feet. I massaged my eyeballs with my fingertips until I felt my head clearing a bit, blinked twice, and managed the few steps over to the door to take the tray from the outstretched hands.

"Thanks," I said, though it felt like I was trying to speak with a mouth full of cotton wool. The hands retreated and I heard footsteps walking away, echoing off the steel walls. So, I wasn't being let out yet, but it could only be a matter of time.

Once I'd eaten and taken a big chug of water, I started to feel better. What would be my next move? Once I got out of here, that was?

Well, obviously, I'd have to act shocked that Jasmila was

dead. I didn't think anyone would suspect me. Why would they? I'd shocked *myself* last night with what I was capable of. No one knew that Jasmila had psychic abilities either, she seemed to keep that well-hidden. There could be absolutely no way that people who knew nothing about how my gift worked were going to make the connections.

That didn't stop me from getting more and more paranoid, however, as the hours dragged on. What was happening up there? I didn't have a clue. This underground space seemed to be well insulated, and all I could hear was the noises in and around my own cell. The gurgling of water in a pipe, the faint thrum of electricity. There were rhythms there if I let myself tune into them.

I became lulled into a sense of inertia as my frazzled brain wore itself thin on the same questions going round and round. I could still hear the rhythms, and they seemed to become one miasma of sound, until finally it all faded and I found myself back in that white space, where I'd shared such useful conversations with the people who shared my gift.

This was drassic. Maybe I could get some helpful advice from my friends. Advice on what, I didn't yet know, because I had no clue what was going to happen when I got let out of the cell or even if I was going to be let out at all—maybe I'd been totally forgotten about—but I'd always felt better about everything after our chats before.

No one was making an appearance, though. Not Kinfala, not Mauritz, just totally blank space all around me. "Hello?" I shouted. I tried walking a few steps in a random direction, not even stopping to marvel at the fact there was no solid ground beneath me, but I could step on this empty space perfectly fine. I was too freaked out. The whole point of this space was to commune with others who shared my gift, whether they were living or dead. It didn't make sense if I was here totally by myself. I could do that in my cell.

After a few more steps I decided to stop and head back the way I came, just in case that made any difference, but as soon as I turned round, I yelped in surprise because now there *was* someone there. Then in the tiny fragment of time it took me to register who it was, my blood congealed in my veins, turning into a sticky, heavy flood of tar that stopped all movement.

Jasmila smiled, but it was a sickly, crazed grin with no emotion, the sort you might get from a murderous clown. She still sported her bandages, now spattered with blood. Her eyes were totally dead, giving off nothing—no anger, rage or thirst for revenge, which only made them more utterly terrifying. And her throat was a livid mess of dried blood where she'd cut it, gaping like a second mouth. Blood spattered the front of her purple nightdress, but my eyes were torn back to her throat—this was where all the anger was. I tried to speak but the words died in my own throat, only a strangled gargle emerging.

She took a step towards me, and I jumped back on instinct. Her grin twisted up at one side, becoming even more deranged, and when she spoke her voice was a distorted, nightmarish parody of her previously well-spoken tones. "I know you did this, you know," she said, her eyes seeming to pierce straight through my skull. "Did you really think you were being that careful? Oh, I knew you were there, you little parasite. It takes a lot to get one over on Princess Jasmila. But I tolerated it. After all, who are you? Insignificant, a maggot. I would have got away with killing him. Ensured that I did. But somehow—and I despise myself for it—you caught me with my guard down. Yes, I am capable of feeling emotion. Okay, so his brother meant nothing to me, but Nathaniel was a good man. Good to me in ways a virgin like you can only imagine," she leered. "I let myself feel an ounce of remorse, and that was my mortifying weakness. I let you slip in. Make no mistake, you will pay, and *everyone* will know what you did." She grabbed my wrist, and I shrieked in pain—it felt like an iron vice was clamped around me, deadening the nerves and threatening to snap the bone. But I couldn't look down. Those eyes had me pinned yet more firmly. "A stupid little girl like you going up against Princess Jasmila. Imagine it!"

I found myself wondering if I could influence her mind again, just to get her to let me go—but she must have sensed this because she laughed in a sort of strangled way and said, "Oh, no, you don't get one over on me again. I learned my lesson, and now you are going to learn yours. I'll let you go, but this isn't over. I'll get my revenge, and it'll be when you least expect it." She let go of my wrist, and I automatically sucked it, not before I noticed an angry purple bruise forming. This wasn't right, I shouldn't feel pain here, I wasn't really here—but it was so real, so visceral. I looked up, but Jasmila was gone, and the brilliant white transmuted into the dull grey of my cell. I sat up on the bed, gasping, and ran the back of my hand across my forehead. It came off wet . . . sweat was pouring off me. Then I checked my wrist. Not a blemish to be seen.

Of course, because that hadn't really happened, had it? At least not to the physical me. But I knew that place was real, I'd spoken to wonderful people there, they'd told me things I never could have known otherwise. I couldn't have dreamt it. But what had just happened—that had the feel of a nightmare about it. I really hoped that's what it was because I wanted to be done with Jasmila.

But there was more to it than that, wasn't there? I sat on

the edge of the bed and pulled a hand roughly through my hair as I thought about what she'd said. Everyone would know what I'd done . . . I'd pay for it. What if she made contact with someone else who had the gift and told them? Of course, that depended on them believing it because there was no physical evidence to show I was involved. And she'd said it would be when I least expected it. It could be years, I could have a career, a family, and then this comes out. And my life would be over. This would always be there, festering at the back of my mind, ticking away like a bomb—but one without a timer on it.

My stomach felt like it had tiny knives in it, trying to pierce me from the inside out. I forced myself to stand up and take steps up and down the small length of the room. Counting them in synch with the beat of my heart. One, two, three, four.

Okay, so now I felt like I could think more clearly. What needed to happen was that Jasmila's responsibility for the deaths and the mayhem became known. Then she would be completely discredited. Of course, I couldn't intervene in that because how would I know about her notes or what she did in the privacy of her quarters?

But once the staff found her, there had to be an inquiry. I wasn't totally sure it would be obvious that she'd killed Nathaniel and then herself. Maybe it would be viewed as the other way round. But either way, they should be looking for evidence of why this took place, which would mean turning her quarters upside down. Her notebook was there, at the top of the drawer where she'd returned it, and they'd see the names and the figures and put things together easily, just as I had . . . wouldn't they? Jasmila wasn't around to serve trial for what she'd done, but it was important it became common knowledge.

Hopefully, compensation would be offered to the victims' families.

Of course, that was out of my hands. There was nothing for me to do here now, and I just wanted to go home. The people were free from this maniac, and the absence of any further violent attacks would be proof, if it were needed, that what I'd surmised had been right.

But I didn't think I'd ever be clear on whether Jasmila's threat to me was real. At least, not until something else happened.

CHAPTER 17

J ust over a week later, I was back at school. I was given the option of having longer to recover, but that was just giving me longer to dwell on what fate might await me, and I wanted to be busy, distract myself. Also, I had the rest of my life to recover from what my so-called gift had put me through. I'd never be using it again.

Once the bodies were found, a flurry of activity had erupted. It had initially been put down as a murder-suicide, although the inquiry was ongoing. Miriam and I were freed shortly after. I was just glad they hadn't forgotten us, although the fact a prince from the region we were trying to make peace with was also banged up might have had something to do with it. Jasmila's death left the throne without an heir, so an arrangement was made whereby Narbert was sworn in as future king once the queen passed on. His older brother was the heir in Narbrutsi, so that should be a way of keeping the peace even if the marriage was no longer possible.

Our infochips had been reactivated, and the first thing I did was message my parents and explain the whole thing, apologizing profusely. It turned out they'd tracked me to the planet and made it to the palace gates, where the guards had told them I was safe and well and engaged in the mission I'd been hired for. It wasn't entirely true, but I was glad they hadn't been put through too much worry. Miriam's mum had taken an interest after she hadn't returned for a couple of days and got the story from my parents. Their reply was full of relief that I was okay, but it also implied a lot more explaining would be in order once I got home. Oh well. I'd deal with it. The news hadn't yet filtered through about Jasmila's death, so they got an exclusive in that sense. It was the reason I was able to leave, so I couldn't really omit it.

At school, I told the rest of my friends that I was through and done with my gift. They got it, once I explained what had happened as well as I could. Miriam got it more than anyone, of course. If anyone else wanted me to step in and resolve their petty quibbles, she'd tell them where to shove it.

I just didn't want to ever go back to that place again, in case I saw Jasmila, but I couldn't really control my subconscious. Maybe if I let my power go dormant, I wouldn't be attuned to it anymore. It's what my uncle had done. Yeah, there was the thing about her perhaps telling someone else, but I couldn't live my life being paralyzed by fear. If it came to that, I would stand up for what I'd done and own it. I'd seen the evidence, and the whole thing was still being pieced together, but it would be clear soon.

That first day back, I met up with Miriam after last class and started walking home.

"How're you holding up?" she said.

I sighed. "It's just good to get back to normality. I learned a lot about my gift over the past week—more than I ever wanted to know, probably. How about you?"

"Yeah, alright. My mum even gave me a hug, broke down in tears when I got in. That's not normal," she laughed quietly, "but it felt good. Hopefully we'll be closer from now on."

"Yeah." We walked in comfortable silence for a while. "Well, my parents are happy at least that I don't want to use my gift anymore. It's what they wanted all along."

I caught Miriam looking at me sidelong. "And if someone else from the government comes along with some high-stakes mission that the future of the planet depends on?"

I snorted. "Then they'll need to find someone else. At least I know there are others like me now."

I just wished the princess hadn't been one of them.

CHAPTER 18

The next few weeks were bliss. I got a couple of requests to use my gift the first week I was back, but Miriam shut them down in no uncertain terms, and thankfully word seemed to get around that I just wanted to be left alone. It was just nice to exist in a world of normality and not some abstract one where I hung around on another plane or had to burrow into people's minds.

I always kept an eye on the news, of course. The attacks had stopped. Things were peaceful, and Narby looked to have settled into his role as heir. I allowed myself to relax a bit and pat myself on the back for a job well done.

Then one night I was streaming the news with my parents and saw something that made my heart sink to my toes.

"We're getting reports of an attack on the royal household," intoned the robo-announcer. "Two guards were viciously attacked, apparently with a knife. One guard died at the scene, while the other put up a brave struggle and escaped with an arm wound that narrowly missed an artery. According to the reports of that guard, the attacker behaved very oddly. After killing one guard, and during the struggle with the survivor, the assailant's facial expression changed from one of maniacal intent to terrified confusion, and he then dropped his weapon and fled."

This wasn't right. I mean, obviously any attack like that wasn't right . . . but there was something so deeply off about this whole story, I felt a chill pass through every inch of me, and I shivered. There was more to this than met the eye. I didn't know what, but I felt it, and it was all to do with everything I'd been through. Everything I thought I'd left behind.

". . . incident interrupts a period of calm since the death of Princess Jasmila, the heir to the Camzhargi throne, and the appointment of Prince Narbert of Narbrutsi as her replacement. But the attack is different from those that took place before the princess's death, which were perpetrated against ordinary people on the street. This crime took place inside the palace, outside the prince's quarters, and royal sources are forced to conclude the assailant was planning an attempt on the life of the prince himself. A full-scale inquiry has been launched as to how the intruder managed to gain access . . ."

"I thought we'd left all that madness in the past," said Dad.

"Yeah, thanks to me," I put in. I thought it was important to make that point, although I'd been trying to move on from everything. It was the first time one of my parents had spoken about what I'd done or acknowledged it, even if it was in a very indirect way. I was still proud of what I'd achieved and didn't want it to never be mentioned. At my words, Dad raised one eyebrow slightly and tipped his head at me, which would be recognition enough for now, I guessed.

The announcer went on to give a description of the man, who was said to be in his early to mid-thirties, short dark hair, average height. Could be anyone, then. But I knew, in my heart of hearts, this was not just "a man" acting alone, despite what it looked like. After what I'd been through, I knew better than to take anything at face value.

The announcer discussed how there was an inquiry about how the man had got into the heavily guarded palace and then apparently vanished again without being detained. That would be disturbing enough to anyone, and apparently residents of the city were taking additional measures to secure their houses. But my sixth sense was telling me this was not about civilians this time. It was "in-house." This guy had something to do with the Camzhargi household and had managed to get in and out undetected. Why? How?

The news moved on, and my parents chatted between themselves in tones of great concern about the incident, but I slipped away to my room to HangFace with Miriam.

She was the only one I could talk to about what I was thinking.

When Miriam answered, I could see from the background that she'd been sitting in her living room, just like I had been, and her mum briefly appeared in the background as she swung the pad around.

"Hang on a minute, I'll take this up to my room."

When she'd got settled, I dove straight in. "You saw the news?"

"Yeah," she said. "That thing at the palace? Yeesh, that's scary stuff. It gave me flashbacks."

Of course. Stupid me—Miriam had been involved in violence at the palace first-hand. Maybe I should have given her a bit of time to process what had happened now. But then, she'd seemed proud of how she'd dealt with Jasmila, even if we hadn't spoken about it since. "You okay to talk about it?"

"Yeah, yeah." She sounded as laidback as ever, but she looked down for a second, and I saw something haunted come into her eyes, thanks to the pin-sharp 3D display. "But I mean, it's weird. I thought all the trouble was finished when that bitch snuffed it."

"Miriam . . ." I paused. This was going to be hard to lead up to. I'd told her a bit about my experiences, the white space and all, but I definitely hadn't told her everything, not the more disturbing aspects. I breathed out heavily. "Jasmila's still out there. In some form. And I'm sure she isn't finished yet."

Miriam looked from side to side, and then down, all the colour seeming to drain from her face. "But she's . . . she's dead, Harica. What harm can she do now?"

I sighed heavily. "Look, I haven't told you everything about what happened to me. There was too much going on at the time, and I know we've both been trying to move on from it since we got back . . . but people with this gift, their essence can still exist, or something like that, after they die. When I overstretched myself with Jasmila, I went to the white space . . . I mean, there's nothing there, no features, but I met two people, a woman, and Mauritz, remember that guy we read about who I'm related to? And those two people are both dead. They were telling me more about how to use my gift, they were really helpful. And then I met Jasmila there, just after she died."

I shivered as the nightmarish image flashed in my mind

again. "I don't know if I dreamed it or it was real, but I'm not counting anything out with her. Assuming it was real, let's just say . . . death hasn't mellowed her. And she's out for me. Not just me either, probably the whole of her own family, and the Narbrutsi too."

"Sheesh, Harica, if you knew this, you should have told me."

"I know. I just . . ." I paused and breathed out. "I wanted to forget about the whole thing. If I could, you know, just for a while. I felt like I was almost wiped out dealing with Jasmila, and I didn't know when she'd be making a comeback. Maybe it would be years, you know, she'd be gathering her strength or whatever. But this latest attack, it's so weird, it's really got me spooked. And to be targeted straight at Narbert . . . I mean, that's about as serious as it gets."

One side of Miriam's mouth was turned down. "You should have told me she was still out there. She attacked me too."

A coldness crept through me at the idea I could've left my best friend vulnerable and I hadn't kept her in the loop. But I really didn't think Jasmila would be out for Miriam now—she would be a bystander in her eyes. "Miriam, she can't get to you physically, she doesn't have a body. And you don't share the gift, so she can't get to you mentally either. And I think, I mean I really hope, she isn't interested in you at this point. But I'm really sorry, I should have told you everything."

An awkward silence loomed. This seemed to be about something deeper than the Jasmila problem, as big as that was—it was that I hadn't confided in her or told her about something that might be really serious. I was about to say something else, but then Miriam coughed and said, "It's okay. You went through a lot, and I can understand not wanting to talk about it for a while. I mean, I can't even imagine doing the things you do, not even resolving a stupid argument like falling out over a boy at school."

I smiled. "Thanks for understanding. And yeah, I really hoped I could move on, but I can't help thinking there's more to this thing at the palace than meets the eye. The attacker behaved really oddly, for a start."

I waited for her to join the dots, based on everything we'd just been talking about, and my girl didn't let me down. "You think . . . Jasmila could be behind this?"

"Exactly. This is not a random attack, there's got to be more to it. I think she's found someone else with the gift, maybe someone who wasn't even aware of it, and she took over his mind. It looks like after she attacked the guards, the guy changed, like he didn't know what he was doing there, and he ran. That means Jasmila fled the scene at the same time. Something spooked her. I don't know what, but Narbert was lucky to escape with his life. But Jasmila isn't done. She'll come back to finish the job and whatever other chaos she plans to cause. I mean, I doubt she would stop at Narbert."

A steely resolve came into Miriam's eyes. "You've gotta stop her. Do whatever it takes. And I'll do whatever I can to help."

I smiled softly. "Thanks. I'm glad you're not mad at me."

She shook her head. "It's fine. I understand your reasons, like I said, and there's no time to be mad. We have to deal with Jasmila, dead or not."

"Yeah . . ." My stomach clenched at how enormous that task seemed. But there would be no ducking out of it now, we had to tackle it head on.

"So, how would she find someone else with the gift, if they weren't already known to her? Is it like a radar she can put out? Or would she find them through this white space?" Miriam was projecting. But that was my girl—give her a problem and she'd set about brainstorming, trying to come at it from all angles. It worked a lot of the time, but this time there was so much that was unknown—even to me, and I had the gift.

"I don't know. I mean, I was there, and I didn't suddenly know about everyone who shared the gift. But I wasn't looking, I suppose."

She pinched the bridge of her nose between her forefinger and thumb. "You said . . . you met Mauritz there, and he helped you. What if it was a member of her family she found? Would that make it easier to find them, and take over their mind?"

I blinked. It hadn't occurred to me. "Well, no one knew who it was. So, if it's a member of the royal family, maybe he's from some distant branch that hasn't been documented. They might be related only very slightly from years back. Or he was exiled or blacklisted for some reason, which might explain why someone at the level of a guard wouldn't recognize him. I don't know. I think we might have to do some digging around this."

She grinned. "I'm up for a bit of detective work, so count me in for that."

That was the old Miriam. "Great. But we need to be quick about it, because we don't know when she's going to strike again."

CHAPTER 19

We agreed Miriam would come round the next night after school so we could start digging around any lesser-known outcrops of the royal family. Miriam was known to be a bit of a techno whiz in terms of getting around the deep web, so hopefully we'd find something, although we didn't have a name for the guy who'd broken into the palace, and it all felt like a bit of a long shot. School was tortuous that day—it was like I'd tried to return to normality, but it was clearly all a sham. I should have known I'd get dragged back into all the madness. I just went through the motions, then we went back to mine after school and fired up the webcrawler.

"Okay, so we'll start off with the classic family tree," said Miriam. "You've got King Finarka, who died in 2561, Jasmila's mother, the queen, and Jasmila herself. Of course, she's an only child, so we've got to look at her grandparents, aunts and uncles. All documented, as far as I can see."

Sitting beside Miriam on the bed, I looked at the vivid 3D tree that was projected, with its various outcrops and sub-branches. "Yeah, these are all names that I recognize.

This is the official stuff, so how would you go about finding someone who'd been cut off somehow?"

"Good question." She tapped in a few commands on the floating keyboard that projected under the image. The intricate tree was replaced with a readout of scrolling numbers, shifting and blinking. Miriam used her hand to scroll through them, moving this way and that.

"This mean something to you?" I asked.

"Yeah, I mean I recognize the commands, but there's nothing that's really adding up. It's just outputting gibberish, really. This represents documents, birth certificates, land registries. But it's hard to see anything that would link an outsider to the royal family."

I let out a heavy sigh. "Thanks for trying. But this is just reaching. It's just a guess that Jasmila's related to this guy, and obviously we don't even have a name."

"I'll keep looking for a bit." A few minutes passed during which I let Miriam work in furrowed-brow concentration, but then she huffed and said, "This is going nowhere."

"That's annoying. I thought I was onto something with this idea about sabotaging the royal family using a distant relative who might hold a grudge."

"It might still be that," she said, turning away from the impenetrable display and looking at me, "but maybe they covered their tracks really, really well in terms of the paper chain from this guy to the core family."

"Maybe. But that doesn't take us further forward."

Miriam hunted around a bit more, but evidently, we were hitting a wall. An idea formed in my mind, something that had been lurking away at the back, but it was going to have to step forward as our number one candidate to find out what was going on.

"I could try and get into her mind again . . . pick up the signal," I said. "Obviously, she's still out there somewhere."

"Is it safe?" she said, starting to shut down the shifting display. "I mean, she nearly broke you the last time."

Yeah, it felt like jumping into a volcano or something, but I couldn't see another way if I wanted to finish Jasmila once and for all. "I think . . . if I go softly at first, don't give myself away. Then if it looks like she's using that guy again, or anyone else, I can try and stop something before it happens. Warn the prince, warn the security at the palace."

"How do you know it'll be the palace again? She might be planning some other craziness."

I looked down at my hands. "That's a possibility, but . . . I just think she's furious that she died before she got the chance to become queen. Revenge is what's most important to her right now. So, while she might get a thrill out of killing some random people on the street, it's not going to satisfy her, ultimately."

"Okay. Well . . . just be careful. Are you going to go after her tonight?"

"I mean, yeah, I should." I had to say, I wasn't crazy about the idea of leaving myself open and vulnerable again, but it was the only way, as far as I could see. *If* the princess was behind it, and *if* she could be stopped . . . yeah, there were a lot of *ifs* involved, but I had to embrace the uncertainty and ride this wild hunch if I was going to save more lives. There was no one else who could do this job.

"I'll go then, before it gets later. Best of luck." Miriam was speaking, but I now only heard the words distantly as a fog of apprehension came over me.

"Okay, thanks," I managed. "I'll . . . let you know what happens."

As Miriam left, I tried not to think about the idea it

might be the last time I spoke to my best friend. I still didn't know everything that Jasmila was capable of. If she detected me . . . would I make it out of this alive?

I laid back on the bed and let myself relax. That took some effort as I was still jittery from the prospect of this mission. But it was the only way I was going to reach the white space. I had to tap into that spectral energy now—it was the best way of getting to Jasmila, picking up her signal.

To let my body shut down, I concentrated on each part of me, starting at my toes and working my way up, letting each part go numb. It was a trick I'd learned when I was younger, after suffering panic attacks. It worked and, when I could no longer feel my body, I focused on my mind.

Slowly I drifted into a semiconscious state, allowing my mind to wander and operate on a more primal, basic level. Although I didn't know how much time passed, I soon found myself in the white space, where I could detect the rumble of other minds similar to mine. That was different from the first time I'd been there, when I'd only been able to go on voices and sights, meeting Mauritz and Kinfala.

I had to tune out those other minds, though, so I could lock onto Jasmila's signal. Her essence might not be actively in this space, because I'm sure she wouldn't come here unless she had a purpose for it, like when she'd threatened me that last time. Presenting with her throat cut, there was no need for that, was there? Any physical manifestation here wouldn't have wounds or blemishes. She was just trying to scare me. Yeah, it had worked, but I wasn't about to admit that to her.

So yeah, I didn't think about whether I was about to

come across her "in person" up here, but this place acted as a database for all those who shared this gift. It should lead me to her, unless she'd changed her signal or something to keep me out. Was that even possible? I didn't know, but I was hoping that in her arrogance she didn't think I would dare coming after her, that I was too scared after the last time.

I could admit to myself that I was, but if I didn't let her see it, that was half the battle.

I found her signal after wandering around for a while, metaphorically speaking, and chasing up various false leads. It was faint, though. Clearly, she was dormant, keeping a low profile until it was the right time to strike. That was going to be a problem. I couldn't predict her moves, and I couldn't be in this space all the time. Her signal was there, but it was just a wisp, an essence—obviously I couldn't see through her eyes like I could when she was alive.

Frustrated, I came away and let myself come back to the real world before I was detected. I lay on the bed for a while longer, allowing feeling to come back to my extremities, before getting up and pacing around the room for a while. I had to figure another way through this because I couldn't watch Jasmila's moves all the time. I had to eat, sleep, go to school, all those annoying everyday things. Massaging my temples, I tried to think. What if there was a way I could keep her signal in the background so I would notice if anything changed? Kind of like an alert?

I could do this. I knew her signature really well by now, I'd locked onto it enough times. She was arrogant, not bothering to change it, not thinking I'd be after her. Maybe I didn't need to go through the white space to get to her.

To practise, I tried walking around my room doing simple tasks, like checking my schoolwork and making my bed, while looking for her signal. At first, I couldn't do it, but then there it was, faint as it had been while I was lying on my bed, but definitely there. It was actually like I had to relax and *not* be actively looking for it before it would appear to me. Okay, so far so good . . . I tried doing something more complicated, bringing up a maths equation in the air above my pad. I allowed myself to concentrate on moving the symbols and numbers around with my finger, and when I took a short break to check on Jasmila, her symbol was wavering a bit, but it was still there. It was important that I was still able to keep her in check while going about my everyday tasks, and I had a full day of school tomorrow.

Okay, I've got you on lock, now let's see you try something.

Satisfied, I went to bed. The only thing that worried me was I wouldn't be able to stop her from killing someone else. But I'd deal with that as and when it came to it.

CHAPTER 20

I met up with Miriam before classes the next day and told her about my plan.

"So, you've got her there, like, all the time?" she asked, peering at me like she could see inside my head.

"Basically, yeah. I check every now and then to make sure I haven't lost her, but I've got to carry on with my day as normal. Then she's less likely to sense an intruder. It's like I've got her on my shoulder or I'm carrying her around in my pocket."

"That's some pretty drassic skills you've got right there," she said, nodding. "After knowing what she did, I think I'd end up sick in the head if I had to spend all that time in her company."

I grinned. "It's not that bad. When she's not actively causing mayhem and she's keeping a low profile, it's just like a pulse, a life force, that anyone would have, although I am getting a faint vibe of malice. I'm just worried if she does try anything while I'm at school, I'll end up zoning out and then have to explain what I was doing to whatever teacher it is."

She elbowed me playfully in the side. "Hey, let's just hope it's during one of Mr Crustallyn's geopolitics lectures then, because nobody would notice. Everyone's comatose in that class anyway."

Rolling my eyes, I said, "Yeah." That would actually work pretty well. But knowing my luck it would probably come at a much more inconvenient time, like if Mrs Hangnaga put me on the spot with a question about the Second Interplanetary Wars. She liked doing that to people. But Miriam had made me feel better, like she always did, and I was glad to have her around.

"Well, it's time for the three of us to get to class. Virtual Technology first," she said, hoisting her bag on her shoulder.

"The three . . . Oh, yeah. Okay." We walked off side by side. And she was good at normalizing stuff, too.

▭

I got through the rest of the day, somehow, although I was pretty jumpy. I needed to learn to not let my nerves get the best of me. There were a couple of times when I thought I felt a shift in Jasmila's signal, but maybe it was just eddies, fluctuations, or like when someone turns over in their sleep. I was just glad I hadn't missed anything yet. I'd have to be patient and learn to live with this because it could be days before she struck again. What if it was weeks? Or months?

Whatever. I'd be here ready if she tried anything. I wasn't about to let this go now after everything she'd put me through.

I walked home on my own after school because Miriam had some sort of club. I normally streamed music through my ear chips, but today I was walking in silence. Even though I was trying to keep things normal, maybe it would be good not to have too many distractions.

Then I felt it. As I was nearing my house, there was a slight shift in the signal—it changed shape, enlarged and became active. Jasmila was on the move. Then I registered another blip, and suddenly there were two signals, the new one much weaker, because obviously she was riding piggyback and commandeering this other person's essence. I had no way of knowing if this was the man who'd shown up at the palace the other day, but I tried to take note of everything I could about the weaker signal so I might recognize it again.

All this while trying to keep one foot moving in front of the other. It was getting harder. The air seemed to be pressing down on me, my eyes watering and my vision distorted. Man, how I was glad this hadn't happened in trigonometry. But my house was in sight, I was nearly there. In my mind, I could see what the host mind was seeing—but it didn't obscure my vision, it was kind of overlaid over the street in front of my eyes, and when I squinted and focused, I could see it better. I made it through the gate into my front lawn and promptly collapsed.

As I lay there in the artiturf, a passing thought was that I hoped nobody saw me and thought I was in trouble—but hey, it was my own house, my garden, and I could have been laying there soaking up the late summer sunshine for all anyone knew. Now I didn't have to worry about the whole walking bit, I gave myself over to the minds inside me so I could see what Jasmila was seeing. I was in a small, poky room—clearly it was a smart home like the one I was used to, but the plastic walls were chipped and worn, even cracked in places, exposing the sensors beneath. It was hard to tell if they were working because I couldn't really register temperature when I was hitching a ride like this. Sound and vision were my two main sensory inputs, but it was clear this home had seen much better days, and if this was some kind of estranged or distant royal like we suspected, they were a long way removed from the comfort and opulence of the palace.

The person had been sitting watching a news readout at the other side of the room, but now they got up and started walking—tentative, clunky steps, because obviously this was not of their own free will. Jasmila was finding her footing. There was a foggy mirror on the wall, which confirmed this was a man of a similar description to the one we'd heard about—average height, dark brown hair, all pretty nondescript, but I'd bet my life that this was the same guy. If Jasmila found something that worked, I was sure she'd ride it out for as long as she could. In the reflection, I saw the man give a sickly grin, and I caught a glimpse of Jasmila in his eyes that chilled me to the bone—the evil, the malice, it was all there, giving me flashbacks to that last ghoulish encounter in the white space.

I checked myself. A visceral reaction like that could give me away, and I had to remain out of sight. Jasmila had moved away from the mirror, thankfully. The guy's feet were moving with more assurance now, and we were out of the room, down a dingy hall with more exposed circuitry, and out of the front door. I tried to take note of where we were, in case I needed it for evidence, but it was impossible —it wasn't like I could make her start going through the guy's data to find the address, and the outside revealed an unfamiliar street that could have been anywhere. I assumed we were down on the planet, and the weather was just as nice as it was up here, so at least I could clearly see what was around me.

What I saw was a pretty rundown neighbourhood, indicating it wasn't just that one house that had seen better days. I was sure the street had been nice when it was first developed, but the coating on many of the squat, single-storey buildings was discoloured, there were more cracks visible, and the road itself was covered in sloppy graffiti that had probably been inked by bored children. I supposed the degradation was something I could remember this street by, but there were probably loads of areas like this on the outskirts of the city. Was that where we were, some kind of suburban no man's land?

I had to process all this while Jasmila was walking the man purposefully towards a beaten-up car parked a few steps down from the house. He pressed his palm to the sensor, the door creaked open, and he piled in, the movements not feeling entirely natural. At least I'd had time to notice the code number on the back of the vehicle, and I did my best to memorize it. The car hummed into life when he pressed his fingertips to the screen in front of the navigator's seat, although it wasn't instant, taking a good few seconds to fire itself up. After he patched some coordinates into the map that appeared, he sat back and folded his arms, and we were off.

"Good afternoon, Raul, it is good to see you again," piped a syrupy female voice into the space. "We will reach your destination of—the Royal Palace—in approximately twenty-three minutes."

The name of the destination came in a stiffer, more robotic voice that jarred me because now my suspicions were confirmed. This had to be the same man who'd already been caught at the palace, but Jasmila must have some brass neck to try the same stunt twice. Patrols would have been stepped up, and they'd be on the lookout for this guy now.

But I had no doubt she'd be bringing her A-game to pull off whatever sickness she had in mind. If that was the case, I had to be A-plus if I had a hope of stopping any of it.

While we glided down streets that became progressively more affluent as we neared the city centre and the palace, I tried to probe around Jasmila's presence while keeping my touch as light as possible, trying to parse her intentions, but she was staying tight-lipped, metaphysically speaking. I guessed she'd be trying to keep the man she was using as a vehicle in the dark too, basically using her entire life force to take over his mind so he wouldn't get an inkling of what was going on and try to mount a resistance. The poor guy. If he got caught this time, he'd be looking at incarceration—or death—for something he had no control over.

So, with Jasmila giving nothing away, I had nothing to do but hold on for the ride and hope I could react to events before they escalated into more carnage.

The car found a parking space that was quite some distance from the palace. I guess that was the nearest it could get. I could just see the corner of the imposing building past rows of shops, and the streets were thronged with people. The palace had always attracted tourists, I guessed, but there'd probably been an upswing in numbers since the attacks on the street had stopped. Maybe people felt safer now the violence was happening inside the palace itself, but they weren't aware the man who'd committed the last attack was now walking among them. He strode blithely down the street, threading through groups of people, oblivious to the muttering and sharp looks he received. Jasmila's arrogance seemed to emanate into the air, and I wished I could warn the people, have someone inform security at the palace, anything.

All too soon, the palace grounds opened up in front of me, a scene that was familiar after my time spent down there. I could see there were extra patrols up and down the fence, but I didn't know what Jasmila had planned. They'd all be on the lookout for this guy, and there would have been security images captured, surely?

The first patrol, consisting of two guards, seemed to be sleeping on the job as the man walked straight past them. Then, as he approached the second pair (and still some way off from the main gates), one nudged the other and pointed.

I groaned inwardly. Who was training these buffoons? They could do with learning some lessons in the art of subtlety. Now Jasmila was forewarned they'd seen her coming.

One of the guards stepped away from the fence to block the man's path. "Excuse me sir, could I enquire as to your business here?"

The man stopped and looked at the guard, who stared back stone-faced, although I could see a trace of fear in his eyes. He probably wasn't paid enough to deal with this. I could sense Jasmila sizing him up, probably judging him as worth less than the dirt under her feet. A few beats went past before the man spoke, in a stuttering, strangled way:

"Y-you have to l-let me pass. The p-prince is in grave danger. I have to warn him."

The guard narrowed his eyes. "Don't make another move. You were caught on camera in the palace two days ago, and you killed one of my colleagues." He pulled out a crun gun, and to my surprise, I felt the man putting his hands up. He didn't say another word but allowed himself to be restrained and led away. They took him to the gates at the side of the palace, through a small door, along corridors and to a cell in the basement—which was familiar because Jasmila had imprisoned me in one that was very similar.

My vision wavered a bit as we walked, and it was clear that Jasmila had turned down the volume a bit. She was still there, but more in the background. This didn't feel good at all, because she wouldn't have allowed herself to be captured without it all being part of her grand plan. Basically, she'd infiltrated the palace, and all she had to do was wait for the right moment to strike. As the man stood in the cell, my vision wobbled again, and I found myself staring at my bedroom ceiling. That meant she'd left him again, for now.

I jumped up from the bed, but then stood there, indecisive. I could wait for the next time Jasmila invaded the man's head and tried something, but I couldn't guarantee I'd be able to stop it. No, I had to take action before that. I had to go after Jasmila while she was on this rest time, or whatever it was, and crush her before she could do anything else.

I didn't yet know how I was going to do that, but right now, it felt like my only option.

CHAPTER 21

The next day, I chatted to Miriam about it over lunch. I could still feel Jasmila's presence as a low-level buzzing, and I was getting pretty good at doing other things without constantly checking on her. I'd have to be, or day-to-day life was going to be pretty difficult.

"So, you basically want to snuff her out completely? Her essence, her spirit, or whatever it is, as well as her physical body?"

"Yeah. That won't be easy, I'm sure, but it's the only way to stop all the madness."

"Is it even possible?"

I pushed food around my plate. "I don't know. Maybe we have to know more about how these spirits work . . . how they present themselves. Are they souls? When she was alive, Jasmila did a pretty good job of appearing like she didn't have one."

Miriam almost choked on a piece of spoonfish she'd just put in her mouth. "Yeah, it was definitely all about the surface, the image, with her. Presenting a perfect façade when what was underneath was nasty."

I thought. The image . . . an idea was taking shape, I just had to find some way of grabbing onto it. "She could present how she wanted to after death too. When I saw her in the white space, she had her throat cut. The people I met told me your essence wouldn't have blemishes, so she presented like that to scare me. Unless it was a hellish nightmare, but I don't know. It felt very real."

"She wanted to scare you . . ." Miriam pushed her plate away and drummed her fingers on the table. "Didn't you say she was coming for you, like she'd let people know somehow that you killed her? Not that I think you did," she added quickly.

I waved my hand, reassuring her I'd taken no offence. "I don't think I did, but then I don't know. I've gone over it again and again, but the whole thing is a blur. She seems set on getting to Narbert right now, but yeah, I'm definitely on her list."

"Which means we need to act now. To save Narbert's life, and your reputation."

I sniffed. "But I want to snuff out her life force, her very essence. What does that make me?"

Miriam leaned forward, keeping her voice low. "She's already dead. And personally, I don't think people should be hanging round like a bad smell in some kind of afterlife, continuing to kill others. It'll make you a hero, Harica. I mean, you already are one."

I didn't know how Jasmila was planning to smear me, but maybe she was going to use the guy who was languishing in the cells, or someone else whose mind would let her in, as some kind of mouthpiece. Maybe it wouldn't be believed, but it was one more reason, if any were needed, that she had to be stopped right now.

Smearing . . . image. I felt the idea taking a more definite shape. "You were saying it was all on the surface with her. What if we can ruin her image after death? Convince people she was a killer? I didn't push that when it happened, I was just glad it was all over and I was going home. But the evidence is there, that notebook with all the names of the people who were killed, and if I can get people to understand that she killed Nathaniel . . . From what I overheard and what I've seen in the media, it was seen as a murder-suicide, but that he was the murderer. I need to explain that it was the other way round."

"How are you going to do that?" Miriam was looking straight into my eyes.

I sighed. I thought I was done with the big ball we were spinning around, and I hadn't planned to go back there, but I couldn't see another way. "I think I need to go back down to the planet."

Miriam and I continued to talk strategy as we wandered home after school. One thing I knew, I couldn't hang about. I had to get down there as soon as possible, even though the idea felt like rocks in my stomach. Even more so when I factored in getting approval from my parents. I wasn't running away this time—I had to do everything properly.

"They'll have to let you go," Miriam said as we walked under the shade of an overhanging synthitree. "I mean, we're talking about saving Prince Narbert's life. And there's an innocent man locked up who you need to prove is innocent."

"I know all that," I said, grimacing as we emerged into

the sunlight. "But they just want me to forget about the whole thing, pretend my gift never existed. To them, this would be like dragging the whole thing up again. I felt the same a few days ago, but this thing with Jasmila . . . I can't just ignore it."

"It's so frustrating, can't they see this is about something so much bigger than them, than us?" Miriam kicked at a plastic bottle on the pavement. "Jasmila will continue to be a threat until she's dealt with, and you've got an opportunity to do that."

"I know. I guess I'll just need to convince them, but it's one more thing that's getting in the way and wasting time. And also, there's the money. We can't afford transport. Last time it was laid on by the government, but that won't be the case now."

"I might be able to help there," said Miriam. "I've got some money I've been putting aside from work. I was planning to use it to help get through college."

"No, you can't do that. You need that." I knew about Miriam's weekend job as a babysitter, of course, but I didn't know she had a little fund built up.

"It's fine," she said, looking at me and waving a hand. "This is more important right now. I'll be able to get it back, put off college for a year if I have to."

I felt a pang of warmth for Miriam's incredible generosity and stopped in my tracks to throw my arms around her, causing her to wobble and laugh. "That's so amazing of you. I wanted us to start college at the same time though. I mean, for all the issues with my parents, at least money isn't one. They're going to help me out, although I do want to get a job as well."

She pulled back, keeping her hands on my shoulders,

and I saw mischief dancing in her eyes. "Maybe you can put it off for a year as well, but we can talk about that later. Right now, there's a prince to save. One thing though . . ."

"What?"

"I think I've only got enough for one ticket. So, you'd be flying solo this time."

"Oh." That was a blow. I'd been so lucky to have Miriam by my side on the last trip, even if we'd been separated a lot of the time, but I couldn't pass up this opportunity. "I mean, of course I really want you along with me, but I understand. Thanks a million for the offer. You don't have to do it, you know."

She snorted as if dismissing my protest out of hand. "I've seen and felt first-hand what Jasmila's capable of. She might be dead, but she's no less deadly."

Buoyed by the support from Miriam—both emotional and financial—my remaining obstacle was to convince my parents. As I waited for them to return from work, I kept telling myself it was nothing compared to what I would be up against with Jasmila.

A couple of hours later, they were sitting looking at me from the sofa while I sat in the armchair across from them. They were holding hands, which looked like another kind of emotional blackmail to me, like they needed to cling to each other to shield themselves against my decision to once again put myself in harm's way. I wouldn't be put off.

". . . your schoolwork is particularly important right now," Mum was saying. "The exams are coming up and . . ."

I'd had it with this. "Mum, if I need to repeat a year to

do the exams, I will," I interrupted. "I know I've missed a lot. But this might be the only chance I get to wipe Jasmila out for good. She's not going to stop being a threat, even though she's dead. I think I know how to do it; I just need to prove to the people at the palace that the man they've got locked up is innocent—he's a puppet."

"But if I understand it," said Dad, "there's no physical proof, it's all in your head. How do you know they'll even listen to you?"

"They asked for my help before. They know my gift is powerful, it's not like I'm just making this up. I need to explain to them that Jasmila shares the gift and is using it for evil. She kept it well hidden, but everything she did is going to be exposed now. Look, if I do this, I'm hoping it'll be the end of the trouble, once and for all. An innocent man at the palace was killed. Jasmila's in the basement—or, I mean, the man she's using is—and she might wait a few days, I don't know, lulling them into a false sense of security, but I've no doubt she'll bust him out of there, cause more carnage. I need to leave as soon as possible, tonight."

"It can't be tonight," said Dad. "It's getting late, and you could at least take tonight to think it over."

Well, this was moving in a positive direction at least. "I won't change my mind. But okay, I can use tonight to get ready, I suppose. Does that mean we can leave in the morning?"

Mum's brow was set in a deep furrow. She looked to be much more against the idea than Dad was, but they exchanged a glance, he raised an eyebrow, and she said, "Okay. But you've to let us know that you're safe, we want regular updates. We were worried sick when we didn't hear from you last time."

I smiled thinly. "That was because my chip was

switched off. It'll be different this time, I'm sure of that. Thanks, Mum and Dad. You're the bopliest!"

I went over to the couch and we shared a group hug, although it was a bit of an awkward one—they were never very tactile with me. Pulling back, I said, "Well, I'd better go and pack. Thanks again!"

I beat a retreat upstairs and HangFaced Miriam before they could change their minds. "I did it," I said. "I'm leaving tomorrow."

She grinned. "How'd you convince them?"

"No tricks if that's what you're thinking. I just explained to them how serious the situation is, and they seemed to get it, though I don't know if they fully understand. But the main thing is I'm going back down to the planet tomorrow, and Jasmila is going to be put in her place once and for all. Is it alright if you send that money over now?"

"Yeah, of course. You don't beat around the bush, do you?"

I laughed. "I'm totally thankful for your amazing offer. I'm just trying to get organized now, there's a lot to think about. And I'll pay you back all of it, I swear."

Miriam lifted one side of her mouth. "Don't worry about that now. Do you know how much it is for the shuttle fare? And where are you going to stay?"

"I had a look at the return tickets earlier. And I'm hoping Narbert is going to put me up in the palace, like we did last time. He's a great guy, and I think they'll see I need to be close by in case Jasmila tries anything again."

"That's putting yourself in harm's way, though."

"I'll sleep with one eye open—or with my mind open." I coughed. "I'm telling you, I'm totally ready for Jasmila this time, and she's not coming out on top. She's finished."

"That's my girl. Just, please, be careful."

"Always." We sorted the necessary financial transaction and chatted for a few more minutes before Miriam wished me luck and logged off. I wished I actually felt as confident as I'd sounded, but convincing others seemed like half the battle at this point.

CHAPTER 22

D ad insisted on driving me to the spaceport the next morning. "I can take the morning off work," he said. Mum had been tearful and flaky before leaving, and I'd given her another hug, which felt more natural this time. Dad seemed to be acting more chipper and upbeat to offset her dramatics, but when it was just the two of us on the way to the spaceport, things went quiet as we both fell into our own thoughts.

I couldn't help thinking about what had happened the last time I'd made this journey. It was still horrific, but it was important, I guess, because it was the beginning of learning I could do more than what I'd thought with my gift. That whole trip was a hell of a learning curve from then on in. But I was glad that this time, I'd be on a commercial shuttle, there'd be lots of people around me and I wasn't going to be left alone with some entitled flamhead. It didn't mean those memories wouldn't get stirred up, but I wanted to suppress them and focus on the task ahead of me.

The spaceport loomed ahead, sinister and forbidding,

and I shifted in my seat, turning away and looking out my window at the streams of people milling past. A lot would be commuting to the planet for work, I guessed. No way I'd want to do that every day. It was so different from the last time when the place was practically deserted, but I guessed we were hitting rush hour now.

"This place looks worse for wear," said Dad, sitting across from me, leaning back in his seat while the car guided us into an underground holding pen. "I haven't been out here for years, and you'd think they'd have done it up by now, but it's all money, isn't it?"

"I suppose. I was out here a few weeks ago, and it was my first time, but I did think it looked neglected."

"Oh, yes. Of course," said Dad, seeming surprised, like my previous unauthorized outing was something he'd rather conveniently forget. I hadn't told them what happened on that journey, and I was glad of that now. They wouldn't have let me go anywhere myself again.

Truth was, as traumatic as it was, I'd dealt with it by relying on my own powers and nothing else, and that was what I had to do now with Jasmila. It was all training, all experience. Of course, my parents wouldn't see it that way, but I'd proved to myself that I was strong. I just had to hope that I could surprise myself once again.

The car found us a parking space and gently shut down its systems with a hissing sound. It kindly told us we'd reached our destination, as if we didn't know, and finally switched off the 3D map.

Dad looked at me. "Well, here we are. We'd better hurry up or you'll miss your shuttle."

"There's plenty of time." But I felt my skin prickling as we sat in the car doing nothing, so we both got out and headed towards the lifts. I could have made my own way at this point, but Dad clearly wanted to see me to the departure point and denying that would have seemed ungrateful. I was definitely glad I had his support—I needed all the positivity I could get. The conversation between us fell away again, and as we went through the formalities of the security checks and logging in, my mind inevitably drifted to what was ahead of me. I could see Jasmila in the white space again, that hellish, gaping maw in her throat, and blinked twice to dispel the vision. *I mean, come on. So unnecessary.* People's essence after they died didn't need to have any blemishes. It was clearly just to scare me, make me feel guilty, and I couldn't let her do that. I'd have to keep reminding myself she was weak at the core, relying on appearances and reputation to manipulate others and get her own way. My job now was to chip all that away, until there was nothing left, and hopefully that would be enough.

"Well, this is it," said Dad when we'd reached the correct departure portal. "Remember to check in regularly to let us know you're okay. I just wish I knew when you were coming back."

"So do I, but I just don't know yet. I know what I'm up against, but I don't know how hard it'll be or how long it's going to take."

Dad shifted, putting his weight first on one foot then on the other. "Look, I know we've not always been the most . . . supportive, me and Mum, about your gift. And it is a gift, I suppose, it's wonderful. But we have our reasons. And we've always just wanted what's best for you, like any parents."

I was about to answer, but Dad was standing looking at me through hooded eyes, seeming like he was about to say more. While he was opening up, it was probably better just to let him.

"Letting you go off like this, on your own . . . well, every fibre in my body is screaming at me not to let you. Especially if it's to do with your power. It makes me sick that I won't be there if anything goes wrong. You've told us what you're up against, and it sounds absolutely horrific . . . but I know lives are at stake here. I just wish yours wasn't too."

This was the most he'd said about my gift off his own back. I very nearly took the chance to ask about Mauritz and how what happened affected the family, but that might be taking things too far. I had the answers from the man himself, after all. Instead, I let Dad hug me, and he held me tightly for what must have been only a few seconds, but it felt like it was making up for a lifetime. The awkwardness was gone, and I just felt love.

He let me go and wiped away a tear. "Look at me, getting in a state. Embarrassing, right?" He smiled sheepishly, and I grinned back. "You'd better hurry up or you'll miss the shuttle."

"Yeah, you're right." I readjusted the bag on my back and looked him dead in the eyes, seeing nothing but warmth and goodwill. "I'll stay in touch, I promise, and I'll be back as soon as I can."

"Good to hear. Good luck." A final quick hug, and then I turned towards the gate. As I stood in the queue to embark, and then took my seat amid the hustle and bustle of businesspeople and affluent families off on day trips, I still felt the churning in my gut over what I was going into, but a new sense of assurance was rising too. I'd got the blessing from my dad, and it was a surprise how much difference it made.

The trip was uneventful, aside from what was going on in my own head. I watched a movie to try to distract my mind from what had happened to me the last time I'd travelled to Sintrago. I tried to tell myself that this was such a different situation, a commercial shuttle with people all around me. It might not be the last time I did it, so I didn't want this to plague me forever—if all the problems were resolved, planetside trips should be a nice thing, shouldn't they?

It did feel like a weight was lifted when I stepped off the shuttle, though. Not an enjoyable experience. Towards the end, a child had been continually whining in a tone that stabbed itself into my mind, overlapping the movie dialogue coming through my ear chips.

Now I had to get transport into the city. I was lucky that my parents had chipped in some money on top of what I had from Miriam, so I easily had enough to cover the short trip. While waiting at the interchange, I folded and unfolded my arms, finding it hard to stand still. My mind was racing with what lay in front of me at the palace. First, I had to convince them to let me in, but that should be okay, shouldn't it? Hopefully they'd remember who I was, and if not, I could easily explain. I'd already decided that I had to speak directly to Prince Narbert, to let him know who was really behind the attacks on his life and what I thought I could do about it. I had a good feeling about this, based on what I knew about him. He was reasonable, approachable, and totally lacked Jasmila's air of stratospheric superiority.

As I climbed aboard the electrobus, surrounded once again by families, an odd sense of calm descended. I was zeroing in on my mission, the palace was only a few minutes away in this crate, and I knew what I had to do. Just the small matter of confronting the metaphysical essence of a sociopathic princess and banishing it forever from the realms of time and space.

Okay, probably best not to think about it too hard.

Once I disembarked at the city terminus, it was just a short walk to the palace. I threw my bag over my shoulders, raised my head and walked with a sense of purpose and determination. I wasn't sure I really felt it, but I tried to tell myself I did. Things were just as busy here as the packed-out transports I'd been on suggested they would be, and that was good, wasn't it? The planet was becoming a destination for tourists again. Clearly people felt safe to walk around without fear of being blown up, and they must have thought an attack that had happened deep within the palace itself didn't directly concern them. But I knew better. Jasmila had been happy to trade in the lives of her subjects for financial gain, and I wouldn't put it past her to kill more civilians.

I decided to go straight to the main gates, although all three were manned—this wasn't about sneaking in the back door, this was about going straight to the heart of power to root out the sickness that was still plaguing this world. But as the gate came into sight, something shifted in my head and I staggered, grabbing onto the wall for support. The crowd re-routed itself around me, but no one offered to help. This was it—Jasmila was on the move again. Would I get there just in time to stop another tragedy? Or would I be too late?

I saw the inside of a prison cell, the person whose head I was in walking over to where a pair of hands extended through a slot holding a tray of food, the same way I'd received meals when I'd been locked up. I forced myself to come away because although it was important to know what happened next, I couldn't do that and continue walking. Painfully, I refocused on the street around me and its jarring colours and sounds, and forced myself to run to the palace, scenarios running around my head like crazy.

Reaching the group of three guards at the main gate, I staggered to a halt. "It's me—Harica Spindelman, I was here before, to resolve the engagement between Princess Jasmila and Prince Narbert," I panted. "You've got to let me in. Prince Narbert is still in danger, and I think the man you've got locked up in the cells might have got out."

"I remember you—of course," said the lead guard, but he was reading something on his display pad at the same time. "You're right—he got the door open while a guard was bringing him food and knocked him unconscious with his own crun gun. He didn't get far because the patrol heard the commotion and got him back into the cell, but they don't know how he got the door open—they've posted two guards outside his door at all times in case it happens again. How did you know? This all just happened."

"Special powers," I answered quickly. "That's why I was brought here last time, remember?"

"Okay, but I thought—"

"There's no time to explain right now. It's very

important that I speak to Prince Narbert, I'll explain to him what's going on. Is he safe?"

"He's been moved to an extra secure suite, deep inside the palace, behind reinforced titanium doors. Guards are on constant watch there."

"Can you take me to him?"

"It's essential that we stay on watch here." The man looked up and down the street, as if underlining the need to stay on constant alert for further attackers. "But I'll send for someone to take you to him." He tapped in a quick message on his device. "He speaks very highly of you, you know—he says you were the one who saved him from being married to a maniac."

I smiled, but briefly. It was too much to go into with this guard to explain that that maniac wasn't done with Narbert yet. But maybe I could press him for some quick information. "Do they know anything about this man, this attacker?"

"Yes, they performed a mental and hereditary scan to show that he's got some distant connection to the royal family. And from the records we've got, that adds up with this story about an illegitimate birth from generations ago. We've got special investigators working on it. What they're thinking is, he reckons he should be next in line to the throne instead of Narbert, who's an outsider. But he's playing dumb when they speak to him. Acts like he's not even aware of what he's done, and he doesn't seem to know anything about being related to the royal family. So, he's an extremely good actor or he's a total sociopath."

I nodded. All of that made sense to me, even if it didn't to the guard. "There might be a third option . . ." I muttered.

"What's that?"

"Nothing. I need to speak to Narbert."

"Very well. Ah, here comes Magronda to escort you."

A tall, severe-looking guard approached behind the gate —he had small, wide-set eyes, close-cropped hair, and a general vibe of taking no rubbish off anyone. The guard I'd been speaking to unlocked the gate and ushered me through.

"It was good to speak to you, Miss Spindelman. Hopefully you can help unravel this mess for us."

"That's what I'm hoping too." The guard nodded and gave a brief salute, which I had to smile at.

"This way," said Magronda, inclining his head towards the palace. *Okay, I could have figured that part.* Unlike the guard at the gate, who came across like a regular old gossip, Magronda didn't say anything else as he led me across the grounds, through a side door and along a corridor that I didn't remember. This one wasn't as ornate as most parts of the palace—it was more functional, industrial chic, and it ended at a plain steel lift. Magronda pressed the button to go up, and the door whooshed open instantly.

The silence gave me time to think at least. So, no one had been killed in the latest attack, which was a blessing at least. I was sure that was by accident, but it showed that Jasmila might not be as all-powerful as she probably thought. Very good.

Was it just coincidence that this happened just as I turned up? Perhaps, but it didn't seem too likely. She was probably still watching me, seeing where I was at all times, and now that I was here, she was goading me, saying *bring it on*. The thought made goosebumps rise all over me. I didn't like to think of her watching my every step, but was there a way to stop it?

The ride in the lift didn't take long. The door opened, and Magronda stepped out, not checking to see if I was following. We were heading down another corridor that was similar to the one downstairs but going the other way from the way we'd approached. Steel doors were set into the walls at seemingly random intervals, and we turned left and right at various corners as well as walking past other corridors that branched off from this one. I tried to remember the way in case I needed to get back to the lift in a hurry, but I wasn't sure I could. This palace really was a labyrinth.

Eventually we reached a big set of double steel doors with a bar going across them as well as a large wheel. Anyone trying to penetrate this room would need to know the code to do it. The security arrangements were completed by two guards who had a more heavy-duty look than the ceremonial ones outside the gates—they were in full-on body armour. They nodded very briefly to Magronda. I didn't know him, but I guessed he was high up in the power structure—he seemed to command respect instantly.

"Prince Narbert has been alerted to your presence and is happy to speak to you," said Magronda. He actually had quite a nice, soft-spoken voice now I'd heard him say more than a couple of words, which made an odd contrast to his harsh appearance—severely shaved head, cheekbones like cliff faces, and piercing, thousand-yard stare. "If you do not mind, I will sit in on the interview as well."

"Of course," I said quickly, while Magronda punched in the combination to open the door. "It's not an interview, it's just a meeting. Well a chat really. No secrets, I just want everything out in the open—"

I quit my nerve-fuelled gabbling when the door rolled back to reveal Narbert standing there with a broad smile on his face. We'd met before, but I wanted to appear composed in the presence of royalty. He had a more hunted look than I remembered the last time, his eyes not quite showing that glimmer of mischief.

"Harica! How wonderful to see you again. Come in, do, make yourself at home in my little abode. Temporary, I hope."

"Good afternoon, Prince Narbert." I gave a little bow, hoping it didn't look too stupid, and stepped through the door and looked around, while Magronda busied himself with securing it again behind us. Despite the industrial vibe of the door and the corridors we'd been travelling, the room was just as luxuriously appointed as the other royal accommodation I'd seen, with the usual selection of no-doubt-priceless paintings, vases, rugs and so on. A couple of doors led off this main sitting area, probably a bathroom and a bedroom. If Narbert was basically a prisoner here, then he was a very comfortable one.

He motioned to one of the chaises longue, done up in luxurious gold fabric. "Have a seat, do." He took one end and I perched on the other, feeling deeply out of place.

"I'm surprised to see you again so soon, I must say. Though I'm glad you made the trip," he began, sitting up straight and crossing one leg over the other. "To what do I owe the pleasure?"

I guessed he knew anyway, but his politeness made him ask the question. "Well, it's about that man you've got locked up in the basement," I said, picking a small piece of lint off my knee. "I already heard from the guard outside that you've found evidence about him being connected to the royal family—his family were cut off years ago and he's out for revenge, or something like that?"

Narbert nodded, looking stoical, but I could see the fear just under the surface. He'd just taken up the job as heir to the throne and had already escaped a vicious attack on his life that had left one man dead. He must have been wondering what he had come into. "That may well be the case, but if you just heard that from the guard, it can't be your reason for coming, can it?"

"No." I sighed. "This is going to be difficult to explain, but . . . he's not really the one you've got to worry about. He's being controlled, he's not responsible for his actions. He's an innocent man, basically."

"Then who . . .?" Narbert narrowed his eyes, then widened them 'til they looked like they were about to pop out of his head. I would have found it comical if the situation wasn't so serious. I could see him mentally winding back the gears to all the mayhem that had unfolded the last time I was here, and I was pretty sure the penny was going to drop—it just needed a gentle push. "Oh, no. You don't mean . . ."

I nodded slowly. "Yep. Jasmila. She's still out there—*she's* the one who wants revenge. I don't know about an afterlife for the rest of you, but people with this ability, this power, they tend to hang about on this . . . I don't know what you'd call it, an astral plane, or something. Because we have access to that while we're alive. It's how we find each other. It's supposed to be a peaceful place, full of harmony, and that's how it is for most of us, I mean, that's if you're content . . ."

I thought of Kinfala and Mauritz—*he* had never even thought about seeking revenge, despite the violent nature of his death. I shuddered. "But Jasmila has tainted it with her deranged nature. I saw her there after she died, with her throat cut—she just appeared like that to scare me, threaten me, your soul shouldn't show any damage to your physical body."

"How awful," said Narbert, but he seemed distant—I could tell he was lost in his own thoughts. Maybe of what a lucky escape he'd had. I gave him a bit of time to catch up, try to process it all. "So, this man, this intruder . . . he's just a scapegoat?"

"Yep," I said. "Clever, I suppose, although I hate to say it. She found someone who would seem to have a reason to want you dead—although he's exiled, he would actually be next in line to the throne because Jasmila didn't have any siblings or other really close relatives. And the idea is, he saw an outsider being installed as heir and thought, 'that should have been me'."

"Does he have this gift too?"

"I don't know that for sure, but for her to find him and take him over, without being near to him in the first place . . . yeah, he'd have to. I don't know if it was dormant or maybe he wasn't even aware of it. It doesn't look like he fights back at all when she's in his head, and I don't know if he remembers anything afterwards . . . but I would say no, or only very vaguely. It would be good if I could speak to him, find out what he knows."

Narbert screwed up one side of his face. "That's a big security risk."

"I know, but it doesn't have to be in the same room. We could set up a HangFace call between here and his cell."

"Couldn't you find him through this . . . plane of yours?"

That was an interesting idea, but I didn't think it was that easy. "I don't know. You have to know what you're looking for, if you see what I mean. Everyone's got their own . . . signal, you could call it, or scent, or footprint. I don't think it can be disguised. I know Jasmila's because I've been in her head, and that's how I've been able to track what she's been up to. And I think she was able to find him because they're related. But for me, there's so much noise in that space, I wouldn't know where to start tuning into his signal. It's better if we just speak directly—you know, the normal way. After what's happened to him, it might spook him if I try to contact him . . . you know, astrally, and also that might be showing my hand to Jasmila, if she's nearby."

Narbert leaned forward and rubbed a hand over his face. The cogs were definitely in full whirring mode by now. "Okay, we'll get that set up. But there's something you said that was interesting . . . I mean, it's all interesting, it's fascinating. And terrifying. A dead person is trying to kill me, how do you deal with that?"

I raised an eyebrow. "You're taking it well."

"It's all show, my dear," he said, waving a hand. "Inside, I'm paralyzed, but one has to be brave, eh? No, what I was thinking . . . It's interesting that two people share the gift who are related. Maybe that means it's not totally random as to who has it. There must be something more behind it. Do you have any relatives who share it?"

"Actually, I do. A great-uncle. But I didn't know about it until really recently—in fact, I didn't even know he existed until after he died. He was one of the victims of the street bombings, see, an innocent bystander. And then I met him in the white space. Maybe I found him so easily because we're related." I hadn't thought about that before. And, obviously, I met Kinfala too because they were friends and hung about together. "My parents hadn't told me anything about him. They always hated me using my gift, and I never knew why, because all I did was resolve friends' silly arguments, it was nothing dangerous. But when Mauritz told me his story, it fell into place."

I shook my head, trying to avoid the scene repeating in my mind again. "He'd been trying to resolve an argument between his brother—my grandad—and another man and ended up killing my grandad. His son, my dad, was only little. So, when I got approached that first time—you know, to sort things out with you and Jasmila—my parents ruled it out flat. I ended up getting away through deception. I just thought I had to, there wasn't any choice. People were getting killed. Including my great-uncle, which I found out about at the time, although I didn't know what he'd done."

"And if you had? Would you still have come?"

I swallowed and looked down at the floor. "I don't know, but . . . yeah, I think so, because I probably would have thought I could control it better." I had to be careful here—Narbert didn't know all the details around Jasmila's death, and I wasn't even sure about it myself, but I had a strong suspicion that I killed her. "But I didn't know. My parents wouldn't tell me. I found out he was one of the victims, a relative of ours, and presented that to them as a reason to let me go, but they just completely clammed up about it. It just made all of us even more angry, but for different reasons I didn't understand at the time."

Narbert leaned back in the seat, his eyes twinkling with sympathy. "I can see their point of view. You are their only daughter—and there was not only the danger to you, but also the risk that you could endanger or kill someone else."

I'd thought about it over and over, and I hadn't even come to grips with the fact my dad had let me go this time. He must have mellowed about things, or maybe he understood now how strong I was. "I know, but when you weigh it up against hundreds of people being killed, it should be a no-brainer."

"Yes, but . . ." Narbert inclined his head to one side, then the other. "I have no children as yet, but the parental urge to protect their young is incredibly powerful, I'm sure."

"Yeah." I had to give him that one, although it was still hard to swallow. "Anyway, it's great to be able to talk about all this with you, Narbert—I feel like you understand, even though you don't share the gift. But it's not getting us closer to stopping Jasmila. And it's only a matter of time before she tries to strike again."

"Quite right, quite right. Time is of the essence, while we're sitting here gabbling. One question—how are you going to eliminate someone who's already dead?"

My mouth twisted. "That's the big one, Narbert. I'm working on it."

The interview with Jesmond Dander, as I learned the man in the cells was called, set up via a pad the guards had provided, went as I expected. He didn't remember anything about the occasions when Jasmila took over his mind, and he talked about a sense of lost time, saying it was like he blacked out and woke up somewhere completely different with no memory of how he got there. With everything I knew, I had no reason to disbelieve him. Yes, he was a second cousin of Jasmila and his family used to live in the palace, but they'd been kicked out after a scandal involving his father, who'd been selling off some of the family's priceless artworks and statues on the deep web. Jesmond had been a child at the time and had nothing to do with it, but he said he had no interest in seeking revenge or avenging his father. He knew his father—who'd since died— had done wrong, and he was quite happy living his own low-key life away from the palace.

After we ended the call, I turned to Narbert and said, "That's not enough. His word isn't going to convince people he's not behind this. We might try getting to the bottom of how he got into the palace the first time—it must have been Jasmila's words coming through him, spinning out some story, but that doesn't prove he was being controlled. I believe him, but it might seem like, if he really wanted to get away from the family, he'd go and live on one of the moons, or even in a different solar system."

I leaned forwards and looked down at the floor, trying to sort out my racing thoughts. "We need actual evidence that Jasmila has this power, because no one knew about it until I did. She's kept up this clean image somehow, right up to the end—people still think she was killed by Nathaniel who then killed himself, not the other way round. That's not right. If we can blacken her name, maybe it'll weaken her, neutralize her somehow—she won't be able to get away with things anymore if people know what she's capable of. I'm not saying it'll stamp her out completely, but maybe she won't be a threat anymore—she'll just be like a bitter soul, hanging around in the ether."

Narbert was nodding along the whole time, face drawn in concentration. "Okay, I think I know what you're saying. Everything was about saving face for her. If she's exposed for what she truly is—or was—what's she got left?"

"Exactly. Now, how are we going to get this evidence?"

Narbert got up and padded over to the reinforced steel door. If I didn't keep that in my eyeline, I easily forgot he was just as much a prisoner as Jesmond was, because the room was so swanky. "I told you that I would take regular walks around the palace when I moved here—it was on one of those walks I freed your friend, Miriam, and then I met you. Well, the idea of doing that was to get a feel for the place, but for the people as well. I wanted to be approachable and get to know everyone in the palace, not be stuck away in my own quarters."

"Ironically, that's the situation I find myself in now"—he cast a hand around the room and grinned—"but not through my own will. Anyway, one of the people I spoke to was an archivist named Dreghorn who looked after all the family records. The family tree, of course, he makes sure it's not missing any branches—so this Jesmond chap should be on there—but also any documents to do with royal duties, or any programs they've been involved in. He also combs the platforms and the news outlets every day and records everything that's written or said about the family."

"Sounds interesting," I said, and paused. The mention of family trees got me going. "I've been thinking maybe there was something hereditary about the gift—I share it with Mauritz, and it's pretty likely that Jesmond has it too, meaning Jasmila could find him—but I don't think that'd be documented if he left when he was a kid. Don't know, though. Jasmila's kept it a secret, so they don't know she had it. Why's that? In my own family, it was like a dirty secret too—my parents didn't want to talk about it. There might have been something gone wrong in the royal family too—one of her ancestors did something bad, intentionally or not, so she wanted to keep it hidden. Let's see if there's anything in those archives that shows if any of her ancestors had the gift. It's a starting point."

CHAPTER 24

Narbert was still confined to his quarters, or he'd have taken me to the archives himself, he said. "Truth be told, I'm fascinated to see it myself. I've only heard of it from this fellow I told you about. But once all this nastiness is over with, I'll definitely be having a look."

He got in touch with the archives department and spoke with one of the assistants there. "Good afternoon, your highness," said the 3D readout of a young man with thick square glasses and neatly combed hair, wearing a white lab coat. His voice stumbled a bit, and he fidgeted. Despite the crystal-clear display, his eyes were indistinct behind the thick frames. "H-how can I help you?"

"Is Mr. Dreghorn available?" asked Narbert in a warm tone, clearly trying to put the guy at ease. "It is a matter of some urgency."

The assistant cleared his throat. "It's—it's just the usual, he's involved in curating some of the material while we're busy monitoring the platforms. Of course, he always keeps a close eye on us." He glanced quickly to the left, as if worried Dreghorn would interrupt the call. Narbert had said he was really nice, so I didn't know if this assistant just had a nervous disposition or if Dreghorn happened to be a hard taskmaster with his staff.

"I'm sure he can spare some time this afternoon," said Narbert calmly. "Young Harica Spindelman is visiting the palace again, whom I'm sure you'll remember—she caused quite a stir on her last visit."

The assistant raised his eyebrows. "Yeah—yeah, that's right. Lots of commentary about it out there. We had a hard time keeping up with everything, especially the stuff about the princess."

I wondered if what was said about me was good or bad. I'd kept away from it all, pretty much, I didn't want to read about it after living through it. Was there support for the princess out there? If so, blackening her name was even more important.

"Yes, well, I can't say too much, but Miss Spindelman has unfinished business, if you like. What she needs help with could mean the difference between life and death. My own, on this occasion. It's to do with the pesky matter of those attacks on my life and revealing the culprit. After the princess's demise, I was happy to step in as heir, so I'd hate to snuff it and leave this fine household with no one to take the throne once dear old queenie passes on."

The assistant gulped and nodded rapidly. "I-I understand. I'll alert Mr Dreghorn right away." I could tell he was unhappy about it, but with the prince's life at stake, he didn't have much of a choice.

"You're a fine fellow. I'm still confined to a gilded cage here, but you can inform Mr Dreghorn that as soon as the danger is passed, I shall take him up on that offer of a tour around the department. In the meantime, I shall have a guard escort Miss Spindelman down, and if he could meet her at the entrance in around fifteen minutes."

"O-okay. I'll go and tell him now." Just like that, the readout of the jumpy assistant dissolved, and Narbert turned to me and said, "Right, I'll call for the guard and have him take you down right now. I can only hope you find something useful. Good luck."

I nodded. "Thanks, but I don't think this is the hard bit. I'll need that luck if I'm going to stand a chance of taking down Jasmila."

It was Magronda again who took me down to the archives department. The banter between us was still non-existent. That suited me though, as I let my mind wander to what I might find down here and whether it would help me at all.

The ride in the lift didn't seem as long as the one we'd taken up from the ground, so I guessed this department must be somewhere in the middle of the palace. Based on everything I knew, I thought I could draw a vague map of where things were, but it would probably have many errors, and there were still entire swathes of the building I wasn't familiar with. Rabbit warren, much?

We exited the lift onto a corridor I was unfamiliar with, which was slightly different in style again. Not ornate and elaborate like the residential areas, not minimalist industrial chic like the dungeons and the "back-of-house" areas, this was somewhere in between, with plain, kind of queasy, green-coloured carpeting and roughly plastered, beige walls. Doors were plain wood and not the normal high-tech, swishy kind. The whole appearance was kind of run-down but functional.

Still without a word, Magronda strode out of the lift and marched left down the corridor, leaving me to hurry to catch up. The corridor wasn't that long and ended in a door that was slightly larger than the others and distinguished by having a videocom next to it. Magronda put his index finger up to it for ID, and an image of a middle-aged man with fuzzy but sparse brown hair appeared. Was that Dreghorn?

"Harica Spindelman here," barked Magronda.

"Very well, I will let her in," said the man in a kindly voice that had a slight twang to it—I couldn't place his accent, it sounded like he was probably from a different solar system. The door swung inwards, and Magronda nodded curtly to both me and Dreghorn without saying another word, before turning and marching off down the corridor.

"Welcome," said Dreghorn, sweeping an arm in the direction of the room behind him.

"Thank you," I said and stepped through the door before stopping to take in the cavernous space in front of me. I wasn't totally sure what I'd expected—maybe a couple of small offices with workers hunched feverishly over a few computer terminals—but what I saw was a huge area, double the height of the corridor I'd just been in, with huge islands of machinery spewing out reams of digital data that were projected in midair. I recognized messages from many of the platforms I was familiar with. I'd got the bit about feverish workers right—there were two or three people to each island, watching the displays with painfully rapt attention and punching in notes on other readouts. They were looking for, what—patterns, trends? Basically, monitoring the thoughts of an entire group of solar systems, and what did they do with that information? It was slightly creepy to think about. I shook myself back to the moment as I realized Dreghorn was speaking.

". . . keep a record of everything here," he was saying. "Otherwise, things would just disappear into the ether, eh? This allows us to keep track of the thoughts of an entire culture, if you like, and adjust accordingly."

"Adjust what?" I asked.

"Why, the messaging that is put out, of course," said Dreghorn, grinning. "That is not done here, but we feed our reports over to the government and it dictates the tone of news reports, announcements. So people feel that the officials know them and are speaking their own language. The content might come across slightly different in different communities, depending on the prevailing winds of opinion."

My head was spinning. They must be crunching data constantly. Algorithms that dictated how you received the news . . . I didn't know if that was common knowledge, but it kind of made sense. Now I thought about it, I never really criticized anything I heard, neither did my parents. But something Dreghorn said bugged me. "Why don't they do all of this at the government headquarters, instead of feeding information back and forth?"

"You are an astute observer," said Dreghorn, wagging his finger. "Well, originally this was all set up to monitor what people were saying about the royal family, because it was always important to them to uphold a good public image—but it was realized the application could be much wider. And the infrastructure was already set up here, we have just expanded a lot over the years and now we occupy two floors of the palace, as you see."

"Fascinating," I said honestly. Yeah, I'd have loved to find out more about the workings of all this, and if it was used as a way to control the population and keep them happy . . . if so, it hadn't stopped the violent protests from happening recently. But I had a job to do here, I had to focus on the task at hand. "Mr. Dreghorn," I went on, "I'm sure you're aware that I've come here with something specific I want to find out. We might not have much time." I was still keeping a mental check on Jasmila's activity, and she seemed dormant for now, but I had no doubt she was secretly wangling a way to get out of that cell. "It's more to do with the historical side of your operation rather than the current situation, if you understand me."

"Of course," said Dreghorn, nodding vigorously. "Curating the historical records is my full-time job. I leave the day-to-day business to my assistants here, although they need regular checks to make sure everything is tip-top, as it were."

I looked around at the various terminals. All the assistants seemed utterly dedicated to their work, and I hadn't even noticed any turn around at the sound of our conversation. It occurred to me that as mild-mannered as Dreghorn seemed, he maybe cracked the whip hard to make sure everything was running at precision. That was the vibe I'd got from that assistant who'd spoken to Narbert, anyway.

"So, what I need help with is this gift I've got, to resolve disputes by going into people's minds." Dreghorn was nodding along, his face impassive. "Well, I'd like to find out a bit more about where it comes from, if that's at all possible. I've got evidence—well, okay maybe not evidence, but a suspicion—that it's hereditary. Also, Princess Jasmila had it, and I'd like to know where that came from."

At that, his face hardened and seemed to grow pale in the reflected glow of the bright digital readouts. "Come with me," he said, pulling me by the arm, and I stumbled.

"We must discuss this in my office where we are not overheard."

I definitely didn't care for being manhandled, but I could see Dreghorn was spooked by what I'd said, and I wanted to find out why. Was this a state secret? One he kept hidden from even his employees? I didn't see any glimmer or stirring that showed those people were paying any more attention than they had been before, but I allowed the archivist to take me to his office in silence, thankfully without any more physical contact. He opened a door set into the left-hand wall and ushered me through before shutting it firmly behind us and using his fingerprint to seal it locked. This whole surreptitious thing seemed odd, to say the least, but I was prepared to go along with it if it meant getting closer to the truth.

The inside had the same sparse, industrial look as the main room, and there wasn't a desk or anything, but only another computer terminal that was equally as large as those outside, or maybe a bit bigger. There was only one chair, which Dreghorn pushed roughly in my direction and waved at, but I felt too antsy to sit and it would have felt awkward if he stayed standing up, so we both remained on our feet.

"That was all meant to have been shut down centuries ago," he muttered, hitting commands on his screens and not looking at me. The change that had come over him from the friendly, approachable man I'd been speaking to a couple of minutes before was quite something. "But I keep records of it, I mean, I keep records of everything, that's my job. It was never meant to get passed down, it's just a case of managing it when we find it. Here—have a look at this."

A video came up on the screen showing people laughing together in various relaxing settings—at dinner, on a beach, on a hotel balcony at sunset. The clothes were different from the synthetic materials we all wore, marking the video as something out of history. Was it from Earth?

The image cut to a man wearing a dark suit and a colourful tie, something I'd only seen in old films like this. "Wouldn't it be good if we knew what each other was thinking?" he said, showing dazzling white teeth. "That way, we could avoid any unnecessary arguments before they even happen. That's the aim of the innovative program called Mentoscope. You'll always know what's going through your nearest and dearest's minds and can take their thoughts and feelings into account before making the smallest decision—a man would know the best thing to say about a new dress his wife is wearing that she secretly hates, for example." The image cut to a couple in the aforementioned situation, laughing.

I made a face. "Talk about sexist . . ."

Dreghorn shrugged and put a finger to his lips, pointing back to the man on the screen, who'd appeared again on the screen and was continuing: ". . . best thing about Mentoscope is that you don't have to have the program installed to benefit from it. Those who have the program in their minds can go into the minds of others who are engaged in a dispute and mediate to help them find common ground. This is a beautiful approach to conflict resolution because there's no need for words—the interloper feels what each of the parties engaged in the dispute is feeling and works to make connections between them. The way they feel about the problem actually changes, which is so much deeper than just using words. The results from our trials on test subjects so far show a ninety-five percent success rate."

Dreghorn paused the film. "Sound familiar?"

"Yeah, of course, that's where I come in—that's my

ability," I said. "But what's this about a program? I never had anything installed. It's just always been there. I didn't have a choice about this."

"Yep, that's the thing," said Dreghorn, shaking his head. "It should never have gone further than beta testing. Officially, it didn't—they shut the program down before it got out of development. A woman they were testing was trying to mediate a dispute between two neighbours over some land they both wanted to extend their houses on. The thing is, one of the parties' minds was much stronger than the other, and she actually inflamed the situation rather than calming it down. The stronger of the two got completely amped up—it was like she'd created a monster— and decided the best way to resolve the issue was to brutally kill his neighbour later that night."

A vision of the scene between Mauritz, my grandfather and Harlow reared up in my mind, and goosebumps rose along my arms. I shuddered and tried to dispel the image. Although I had a feeling I knew the answer, I asked: "How did they know the murder was linked to the intervention?"

"The murderer had no memory of doing it. That was all the evidence they needed, really—he wasn't in his right mind, wasn't in control of his actions. He came to himself in his neighbour's kitchen with the other man full of holes, three different knives lying around him—no memory of what he'd done or how he'd got there. He turned himself in and waited for the police to arrive. They said, if he'd known what he was doing, he'd have made some effort to conceal the crime. He didn't have a history of mental disturbances, psychotic breaks—he didn't have a criminal record of any kind. Because of the special circumstances, he escaped a conviction of murder, and the public weren't happy about that when it got out."

"When it got out? I take it they tried to cover this all up then?"

"Yes, but even back then the platforms were all-powerful—they were different then, and they called it 'social media,' but then as now, it was really hard to stop things leaking out. Bad news tends to stick. They shut the program down, and there was no further word from the government about it, but that wall of silence maybe created more damage than if they'd come out and been honest about things."

My head was spinning. So many questions, it felt like they were all piling up against each other. But one poked its head out from the jumble: "What happened to the woman who did the intervention between the two men?"

"She was beside herself. Couldn't believe what had happened and saw herself as the true murderer, no matter how much they told her it wasn't her fault. She demanded the program be removed from her head, but that's when they found out it was irreversible—it had fused itself with her cerebral matter, become a part of her. If they tried to remove it, there was a high risk of killing her. She vowed never to use it again, but it kept coming up unbidden—she was freaked out by knowing what other people were thinking, and it drove her mad in the end. She took her own life two years after the experiment."

"Yeesh." I shuddered. Sometimes I'd seen my gift as more of a curse than a blessing, and that was the logical extreme of that. But I guessed some of us were better at controlling it than others. "So, if it was shut down, how come it still seems to pop up so much? Hereditary, yeah?"

"Precisely. I don't know if that was intentional or an accidental by-product—the records at the time don't say anything about it. But they wanted this to be a part of people, part of their DNA, not just a temporary add-on, if you like. Once you've done that, you can shut the program down, but you can't take the power out of people's brains— and clearly, the genetic information of the ability started to fuse itself with the subject's original DNA and became just another hereditary trait to be passed down."

I felt like I was coming some way to understanding this now, but I had so much more to ask. I'd taken a trip out with my family when I was younger to see some of the moon's craters that had been left untouched— others had been filled in to build on, and apparently our own town stood on one. A weird fog filled a particularly large crater because it was still early in the morning when we got there, but Dad told us to wait a while for the sun to burn it away. We sat at the crater's edge while the sun climbed higher in the sky, ate a little of our picnic, and sure enough, the fog thinned out in places so we could see the vegetation and make out a few animals grazing in places. I felt like that now—I didn't know everything about my power yet, but I was getting there, bit by bit.

"So . . . one of my ancestors must have gone in for the trial, then?"

"Must have." Dreghorn inclined his head to one side, then the other. "I'm sure we can find out exactly who that was, if you like."

"I'd like to, but I don't want to take up too much time. Maybe later." The need to deal with Jasmila pressed down on me, and although she was still dormant, I couldn't trust her one inch. I felt like she could come to life at any minute, and if she could figure out a way to get out of that cell, she would. So, Jasmila . . . if she had it, then . . . "They experimented on royalty?" The question sounded slightly random, so I went on. "Sorry, I'm just trying to figure out how Princess Jasmila got her ability. It seems pretty unusual for them to have used royalty as test subjects, I mean, you'd think it would be ordinary Joes."

"I thought you'd get onto that. It was the king himself who signed up for it back then, and it was pretty well documented, as you'd expect. There's plenty of records and clips. I'm sure he was advised against it, but he claimed he wanted to set an example for the people, that this was perfectly safe and it was the way forward for humanity— he said it was the way to stop wars, terrorism, everything. It didn't quite work out that way, of course."

"Hmm." I scratched my chin. "It sounds like he had good intentions, anyway, which is more than I could say for Jasmila. So, random members of the royal family would have had it down the years? Any records of those?"

"Not unless they came forward with it. It's perfectly possible to keep it hidden, and even if they'd mentioned it to someone, like an advisor, it's highly likely they would have been told to hush it up. There'd be bad publicity if people knew or found out how the original trial went down."

"So, Jasmila knew what she was doing by keeping it hidden . . . That's about to come crashing down, though, I'll make sure everyone knows. Meanwhile, this poor cousin chose not to use it at all, and now it's being used against him."

"Yes." Dreghorn nodded slowly. "It makes sense that if you don't train yourself in using it, that means you're more vulnerable to others taking advantage of it. You wouldn't know how to fight back."

"Yeah, figures." I stopped and thought for a minute and realized there was one thing about all this that was really bugging me. "If this ability is such a negative, why did they approach me to help out with an intervention between

Jasmila and Narbert? Weren't they worried something would go wrong?"

Dreghorn threw up his hands. "I've wondered it myself, and I don't have an answer. Maybe they were desperate and felt like they'd run out of options. Maybe they thought you could be controlled, because of your age, and it could all be done in a very safe, managed way. Of course, the factor they didn't count on was Jasmila."

"Yeah, she kept it hidden well. I definitely wouldn't have been roped in if they knew what she was capable of. Well, it all needs to be common knowledge now. I think . . . I think Jasmila was someone who thrived on image. Okay, so she did have a reputation for being selfish and entitled, but I think she kind of projected this regal, untouchable air. If people knew how rotten she really was at the core, knew what she's actually done and what she's doing now . . . . it might help me stop her somehow. I'm not sure how, but it might weaken her. It's not going to satisfy her to commit a crime that she knows she can't get away with."

Dreghorn frowned, making deep wrinkle lines appear on his forehead. "I can kind of see that, but what can they do to her, even if they know it's her? They can't capture her or put her in prison. She's an essence, a wisp floating around."

"I know that, but it's about the image. She's so vain, she wouldn't want that tarnished, even after death. Especially then. In the history books, her legacy would be as a vicious killer, not a beautiful princess whose life was tragically cut short in her prime."

Dreghorn pushed his glasses up on his nose and nodded. "Okay, I'm with you. So, what do you want me to do?"

"Can you prepare a story or report showing what I've

found here, that the gift is hereditary and was passed down to Jasmila as well as this cousin? Like you said, there's plenty of evidence that the old king signed up for the trial. You can make that a part of it."

"I could give it a go, but I'm more of a curator of material, not a *creator*. I could ask some of my contacts who work at the platforms to look into it."

"I'm not sure there's time for that," I said, folding my arms then unfolding them again, thrumming with anxiety. Excitement, too, that I finally had a chance at taking down Jasmila, but it wasn't really full on. Did I have enough? Evidence . . . I'd just said there was plenty of evidence that the old king was involved, but after that it had all been hushed up. No, there was something I was missing here—what had Dreghorn said? It was passed down, hereditary, so . . . I jumped up in the air. Of course!

"You said it fused with their DNA, became part of them, so it couldn't be undone. Well, all they have to do is take a sample of Jasmila's DNA, don't they? How easily can that be done?"

Dreghorn screwed up his face. It was quite a difficult request, I suppose, but I'd presented it like I was asking for an extra drop of milk in my tea. "She's entombed in the royal crypt. You'll know that, of course it was covered extensively . . . She'd need to be exhumed, and I don't know how straightforward that'll be."

"Prince Narbert will authorize it," I said. "He knows how important it is. Otherwise, he'll be next in line for the crypt. We need to get on this today." Narbert was the standing heir to the throne. While he might not have the unlimited power that the queen had, his wishes would still have serious clout—and I'd go to the queen if I had to, although that might be trickier, given it was her daughter that I wanted exhumed, and she didn't know the extent of her deviousness yet. I imagined it might be difficult to swallow, even when the evidence was in front of her.

Before Dreghorn could say anything else, I went on. "Okay, can you call someone to take me back up to Narbert's quarters? I'll explain to him what needs to be done, and we'll take it from there. In the meantime, it would be great if you can start work on that package. We'll stay in touch, and I'll let you know when's the right time to release it."

"Okay, understood."

I smiled. "I really appreciate your help with all this. It's a lot to ask, and I know you're busy here . . ."

He waved off my concern. "I know this is more important right now. It's not every day you get a chance to have a hand in saving the future king."

CHAPTER 25

Two hours later, I was pretty sure I had all my ducks in a row. We'd isolated the genetic pattern of the original program, and a DNA scan of Jasmila's exhumed remains provided evidence that she did indeed possess the ability. I was glad I wasn't there to witness that—it was hard enough dealing with her in the afterlife, I didn't want to look at her carcass as well. I'd thought about getting a scan done on the cousin as well, to show beyond doubt she was controlling him, but she would know something was up then. Hopefully, what she had was enough. And Dreghorn was super-fast putting together material on the hereditary nature of the gift, which included the fact that Jasmila had it. His job was wrangling archive material, so I was pretty sure he enjoyed it.

Now all that was left was to confront Jasmila. Yeah, just that. I had no idea if what I had in mind was going to work, but I had to give it a shot. Still holed up in Narbert's padded cell, I sent the message for Dreghorn to release the film on all the platforms. Then, I got Narbert to turn the lights off and laid down on the chaise longue. I couldn't just zoom in and out of the white space like I was HangFacing with someone, so I had to get the conditions right as well as I could. Luckily, the luxurious furniture was extremely comfy, which helped. A lot better than the rock-hard prison bed I'd had available at previous times.

Closing my eyes, I let myself drift away until the white space materialized around me. There was no one in sight—not Mauritz or Dreghorn. Good, I didn't need distractions. I homed in on Jasmila's signal while dropping my own defences—this time, I didn't care if she found me.

With all my energy concentrated on her signal, while leaving myself totally open, it was like two magnets pulling towards each other with irresistible force. Jasmila materialized in front of me, looking every inch the regal beauty—throat thankfully intact. I still didn't know if that hellish encounter the last time had been for real or if I'd just dreamed it.

"You?" she scoffed. "You've got some nerve coming after me. Yes, you may have killed me, but that doesn't mean I'm finished. You'd better stay out of my business if you don't want to get hurt."

"I didn't kill you," I said as boldly as I could manage, looking her dead in the eyes, where I saw nothing but malice, guile and deceit all mingling in a hellish cocktail. I didn't know if that was true, though. As much as I despised her with every fibre of my being, I didn't think I had it in me to kill, but I'd done a lot by now that I didn't think I was capable of. Did she kill herself or did I push her to do it? The answer was probably somewhere in between.

As if reading my thoughts—which she no doubt was, considering I'd left myself exposed—she made a "tschh" noise and said, "Oh, you did, dearie. I'd never take the coward's way out like that. Nathaniel—well, that was a shame, he didn't have to die, I suppose, but I could have found a way to make it look like something else. I wouldn't have been suspected. Suicide is for the truly desperate, and 'desperate' is not in my vocabulary."

"Well, you might be feeling it after the truth about you comes out," I said evenly. "I know what you've done, and I know what you're trying to do to Narbert. Everyone will know soon."

"Narbert is a fool and upstart," she spat. "He doesn't deserve to be king, he's nothing to do with my family. And once I've dealt with him, I'm coming for you—nobody would believe what you have to say, anyway, but that score needs to be settled. I'm not going to let my murder go unpunished."

I looked down at the ground for a few seconds—or where the ground would be if there was some—and back up at her mocking eyes, so full of scorn and disdain. "They won't need to listen to me. The evidence is there. Did you know that gift of yours is sewn into your DNA—and mine too, and your cousin's, and anyone else who's descended from that first test group? Don't know if you've read up on your history, but your ancestor, the king, signed up for a trial to have the gift implanted. It all went wrong, of course—I think we both know how this thing can go wrong—and they shut it down, but not before the ability had fused itself with the subject's genetics. So, it pops up here and there down the years. You might have hidden it while you were alive, but we happen to have a handy piece of evidence in the form of your pretty little corpse."

She raised her eyebrows. "That's a pretty gross violation, wouldn't you say? And what does it prove? You might be able to show that I had this power, but you can't track what I've done with it."

"Maybe not, but once an idea is in people's minds . . . it has a tendency to stick. You presented this perfect image while you were alive, but it's harder to do that when you're dead. This narrative about an estranged cousin wanting to get revenge, it's flimsy, to say the least. He clearly doesn't want anything to do with it. The truth about what you're capable of is being unleashed on all the platforms as we speak. We also have evidence of your involvement in the street killings—for nothing more than money and so you could paint a picture of there being resistance to your marrying Narbert. There's a lot of grieving families out there who'd appreciate having answers, and now all the fingers are pointing at you."

"You're wrong. I'll still have my revenge," she said. "And you seem like a pretty good place to start."

I gasped and felt myself shake physically as she invaded my mind like a viper springing at its prey. I'd left myself completely wide open and so I didn't have a chance of stopping it. I tried to put up my defences, but it felt like too little, too late. I was a worm trapped under a boulder.

"You did kill me," she said, her voice sounding weirdly distorted and metallic. "I was always going to come for you someday, but seeing as we're both here now, I might as well tick that off my list."

I could hardly move, think, breathe now. She was too strong. This was it. I was going to be killed by a ghost.

I felt myself start to drift away in my mind. Just to get some relief. Then I felt like I was hovering above the scene, watching my own death.

Then it hit me. I couldn't let this happen. I'd come too far to let her get the better of me. And, somehow, I *knew*, right there and then, that I *had* killed her. Maybe I'd been denying it to myself, but I'd done it because it needed to be done. And if I'd done it before, I could do it again.

This was the essence of Jasmila I was dealing with, in the raw. And at the heart of that—what had always been covered up by the trappings and accoutrements of her station—was self-loathing. I'd used it before, and now I needed to do so again. She was suffocating me, but I managed to find a tiny space to move and, once I'd got a bit of traction, I pushed with all my might, the effort making me feel I was going to turn myself inside out.

She sensed my defiance and redoubled her own pressure, but I wasn't going to give up now. All that was left was her core, and it was rotten. If I kept pushing, surely it would crumble.

"See, I think you thrive on image and reputation. But it's all surface. Money? Gold? Dresses? You don't have a use for those now, so all that's left is yourself. And that's too much to live with."

Looking at her form in front of me, it was wavering and flickering, like a poor signal on a HangFace call. This was it —the veneer was cracking.

Her features were dimmed to me now, but I made out her opening her mouth to say something—but before she could, she winked out completely.

Total nothingness surrounded me. It was an immense relief after the mental strain of dealing with Jasmila. I checked for her signal, but found nothing at all—and already, I was struggling to remember the shape of it, the feel of it.

I'd done it. She'd vanished into oblivion.

The white space dissolved around me, and I blinked, finding myself staring up at the ceiling of Narbert's quarters again. Well, that was it. I didn't know when I'd be using my gift again, but I'd learned one thing: it was part of me, and there was no use trying to pretend it didn't exist. Only I'd never let it get out of control again. I'd use it for the right reasons, when the occasion demanded.

I owned it, not the other way round.

ABOUT THE AUTHOR

Nick Wilford is originally from Brighton, England and now lives in a quiet town in Scotland with his wife, three daughters and six rescue dogs. Wanting to make a career from writing, he trained in journalism, but soon realized that the fictional realm was where his true passion lay. He enjoys writing speculative fiction, exploring the things that cannot be seen and "making the impossible reality." Nick is the author of the *Black & White* YA dystopian series and has also published a collection of shorter fiction as well as curating, editing and publishing a fundraising anthology featuring a diverse array of talent. By day, he works as a freelance editor, and he also enjoys travelling to inspiring locations with his family, listening to music and helping unwanted dogs find loving homes.

ACKNOWLEDGMENTS

A huge thank you to my insightful critique partners, Annalisa Crawford and Rebecca Douglass, whose invaluable feedback helped me elevate this book from promising into something I am truly proud of.

Thank you to Jean Lowd at Creative James Media for being such an enthusiastic champion of my book and responding to it so quickly and positively. You've given my book a great home.

Thanks to my superstar editor Staci Petroski for helping me sharpen Harica's story and take it to the next level.

Thanks to my wife Heather for reading the manuscript and giving excellent suggestions on tone and phrasing for my teen characters. The dialogue reads a lot more naturally now. I appreciate you babe!

Finally, thanks to the Insecure Writer's Support Group and all the friends I've made in the author blogosphere over the past decade or more. Without your constant encouragement, advice and cheers, I wouldn't be the writer I am today.